A STRANGE WOMAN

A STRANGE WOMAN

LEYLÂ ERBİL

Translated by

Nermin Menemencioğlu & Amy Marie Spangler

DEEP VELLUM PUBLISHING

DALLAS, TEXAS

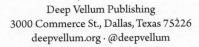

Deep Vellum Publishing
3000 Commerce St., Dallas, Texas 75226
deepvellum.org · @deepvellum

Deep Vellum is a 501c3 nonprofit literary arts organization
founded in 2013 with the mission to bring
the world into conversation through literature.

FIRST EDITION

Support for this publication was provided in part by grants from the National
Endowment for the Arts and Amazon Literary Partnership.

LIBRARY OF CONGRESS CONTROL NUMBER: 2021950665

ISBN (TPB) 978-1-64605-148-9
ISBN (Ebook) 978-1-64605-013-0

Cover design by In-House International Creative
Interior Layout and Typesetting by KGT

PRİNTED İN THE UNİTED STATES OF AMERİCA

Translator's Preface

A *Strange Woman* caused quite a stir in Turkey upon its publication in 1971. Uproar greeted the book's frank depiction of a woman's quest for liberation, including the sexual kind, and its treatment, without mincing words, of such taboo topics as virginity and incest. In the years since, the novel has risen to the status of modern classic, a pioneering work of feminist fiction.

The book's title has become an epithet for the author herself, whom I would also describe as "strange" in all the term's myriad shades: unusual, out of place, peculiar, queer, bizarre, perplexing, alien. (I would mean this as a compliment and I should hope that Leylâ Hanım would take it as one too. Insofar as I had the pleasure and honor of knowing her, I believe that she would.) And it's true that *A Strange Woman* contains autobiographical elements: Leylâ Erbil came of age at the same time as *A Strange Woman*'s protagonist, Nermin, and like Nermin knew a thing or two about living with an overbearing, conservative mother and confronting, and defying, a male-dominated literary scene that looked upon women primarily as flesh for the taking. Leylâ was a politically engaged leftist of middle-class upbringing, as is Nermin. Like Nermin's father, Hasan, Leylâ's father was a ship captain.

However, the most important projection of Leylâ Erbil onto the page in *A Strange Woman* is that of her conflicted self. Erbil wrote unsettling texts about unsettled people embodying all manner of contradictions, because she recognized the complexity of the self, in her own self and in others. Yet while plumbing the depths of their psyches, she also cast an eye on the social and political forces that shape her characters. The reader may feel the tension of a tug-of-war between the self and outside forces, but also a queasiness at the realization of just how entangled these various elements are—can the self extricate itself from this murky mess, this quagmire, or is it not already too weak, too wounded, to do so?

In this spirit of contradiction, Erbil drew upon two sources that, at the time of her writing, were virtually unspeakable in the same sentence: Marx and Freud. Though a politically active leftist herself, Erbil defied the norms imposed by Marxist circles by taking the human subconscious seriously. For her, the ills of Turkey, of the world, of humankind could not be alleviated through purely materialistic means; the trauma runs too deep. In Erbil's eyes, we are all wounded creatures, and the very norms of our societies reflect this reality. Readers who know this will not be surprised by the stream of consciousness technique seen in the second section of this novel, in which a dying father's mind drifts in and out of aware-ness of the present, dredging up traumas of the past through myriad associations, refracted through the prism of his per-sonal history and the history of his land. It will likewise not come as a shock when Nermin, as a grown woman in the final section of the book, has sex with a certain Joseph, the Stalin of her fantasies.

Another aspect of Nermin's conflicted character is her relationship to class. Suffering from a kind of savior complex, she has to grapple with the apparent impossibility of the task she has taken upon herself and, by extension, with her own ego. While the conundrums she faces are situated within a particular time and place, they transgress both and are with us still. Nermin is the embodiment of the liberal educated elite unable to comprehend why so many of the downtrodden fail to rise up, why they act, it would seem, in blatant contradiction to the interests of their own class. But what does it mean when one simultaneously infantilizes and exalts the other? Is it pos-sible to wag your finger and applaud at the same time?

Erbil's writing career was one literary revolt after another: a series of utterly unique works, the produce of an utterly sin-gular mind. Her rebellion is not limited to the themes she tack-les; it consists in the form and style of her writing as well. Her quest to break through the constricting norms that bind us, the very same ones that wound us psychologically, included subverting the rules of language and grammar. In *A Strange Woman* we see the seeds of what would become trademarks of her writing: two periods followed by an exclamation mark, for example, or the leaps and bounds of the father's mind in discombobulated sentences, mangled quotes, and a cascade of associations. Erbil's grammatical insurgency came to full fruition as her career continued, exploding into heretofore unseen punctuation marks: exclamation points and question marks with commas rather than dots, and perhaps most famously, the comma ellipsis—the swipe of a lion's paw, an indelible mark upon the page. Her writing unleashes words, too, setting them upon the reader in transgressive forms. Indeed, Erbil's last two books would be novels in a kind of postmodern, freestyle verse that could, in part, also be read in reverse.

These are some of the predominant characteristics of Leylâ Erbil's work, the same ones that guided my decisions regarding the translation of *A Strange Woman*. It seems to me fitting that this translation process was, like its author, rather unconventional.

A Strange Woman was originally translated by Nermin Menemencioğlu in the early 1970s. Herself a scholar and already an acclaimed translator of Turkish poetry, Menemencioğlu had come to admire Erbil's short stories and began corresponding with her, eventually asking if she might translate "The Ferry" with an eye to publication. Menemencioğlu lived at the time in London, where she had cultivated an impressive literary circle while also keeping her finger on the pulse of contemporary literature in Turkey. I have had the privilege of reading her letters to Erbil, housed in the Leylâ Erbil archive at Boğaziçi University. These letters reveal a passionate intellectual engagement between the budding, lauded if controversial author and the wise, established translator some twenty years her senior. Menemencioğlu's admiration of Erbil's work only waxed over time so that, after securing publication of "The Ferry," she endeavored to translate Erbil's first novel, *A Strange Woman*. She did so, sometimes debating certain points with the author after getting feedback from British editors. Yet, ultimately, she ended up with a handful of encouraging responses but no publisher willing to commit to *A Strange Woman*.

This translation could have been published in its original form, and world literature would have been all the richer for it. I knew, however, that some changes would have to be made because (given my description of Erbil above, you will not be surprised to learn) Erbil, in typical unconventional form, "updated" the novel for most new editions by incorporating into the section "The Father" newly discovered information about Mustafa Suphi. Suphi, you see, was the founder of the Turkish Communist Party who was killed together with fifteen others during a voyage in 1921, apparently undertaken with the aim of consulting with Mustafa Kemal about possible collaboration. This was two years before Mustafa Kemal would lead the nation to victory in the War of Independence and become Atatürk, "Father of the Turks." One cannot help but wonder how the course of history might have changed if Suphi had not been murdered in an assassination plot that remains shrouded in mystery.

While adding these passages I discovered that Erbil had made some other changes to the text over the years, most relatively minor but some substantial. Unable to help myself, I

9

began comparing Menemencioğlu's translation to the Turkish text line by line and found that the English had been stylistically "smoothed out" in many ways. Knowing what a stickler Erbil was when it came to style, and how deliberate she was in the choices she made, I wondered if the translation shouldn't be further edited. The more I began to compare, the more interventions I made. I did not take this matter lightly, tortured by the question of how much authority I could justifiably exercise. Because both the author and the translator are unfortunately no longer with us, it was a decision that I and the publisher had to make.

As I worked on the English text, several factors alleviated my conscience. First, it was evident from Menemencioğlu's letters that some of the changes she wished to make met with pushback from the author. Second, it was clear that while she certainly had no intention of "dumbing down" the text, Menemencioğlu was struggling to make it as accessible as possible to an English-reading audience, in part on the advice of editors who arguably did not understand the purposefulness with which Erbil made her stylistic choices. Third, knowing the subsequent trajectory of Erbil's prose, I thought it would be a disservice to the author to reduce in any way the complexity of her work. As a translator, I believe it does the reader no favors to simplify for them in translation what is challenging in the original. Finally, a letter that Leylâ Erbil's daughter, Fatoş, discovered on her mother's computer just as I was struggling to determine a course of action affirmed my decision to involve myself more intensely in the translation. It is a letter about a translation of her book *Cüce* (*The Dwarf*), in which she explicitly underscores the importance of form and style in her work and demands revisions to this effect.

I decided to attach my name to the translation because the revisions were so substantial that I did not think it right to attribute it only to Menemencioğlu. I did not completely retranslate the book, but neither was the translation Menemencioğlu's alone. My name, the publisher and I agreed, should be added so that I might bear the brunt of any criticism. I wish only that Erbil and Menemencioğlu were still with us so that we might have collaborated on the text together in real time.

I will sign off with an excerpt from one of Erbil's letters to Menemencioğlu (18 November 1969).* It is a response to Menemencioğlu's request for a biography that she can append to submissions of her translation of "The Ferry":

> I was born in Istanbul in 1931. It was in Istanbul that
> I went to elementary, middle, and high school. I studied English philology for five years at university before
> dropping out. I got married, I have a daughter. Though
> I worked for several years at various businesses as that
> object they call a secretary translator, I never developed
> much of an affinity for anything other than writing. At

---

* This was found among Leylâ Erbil's own letters, and so must be a draft of a letter that we can only assume she sent to Ms. Menemencioğlu. Unfortunately, Erbil's letters to Menemencioğlu have not yet come to light.

the age of 18, in the belief that I was putting up a feminist fight, I began frequenting meyhanes in the accompaniment of male artist friends, and that's how I ended up meeting Sait Faik. Laden with a sense of responsibility that was foisted onto me while I was growing up, despite my aspirations to the contrary, I failed to emerge as one of those full-fledged, drunk-on-life artists! I've also managed to avoid a good part of those things I believed could get in the way of my writing. These days I harbor no purpose other than a passion to write continuously without losing my mind or my soul here within this society, and I have reached the age of maturity. If I'm able to make some money from a play I translated for the National Theater, a book of mine will be published in the fall.

That forthcoming book is *A Strange Woman*.

Amy Marie Spangler
December 2021

Editor's Note

This translation includes explanatory notes that the author made to certain terms in the original Turkish text. Notes from the translators are marked (*t.n.*).

PREFACE TO
THE SIXTH EDITION

There have been a few changes made to the new edition of this novel. As in nearly all my books, in this novel, too, I have, for reasons I deem necessary, made small redactions that do not alter the essence of the novel, and in this case I have felt it necessary to use some information and documents I have newly become aware of regarding Mustafa Suphi.

And so it is my hope that those like myself who have been somewhat obsessed with the "M. Suphi Incident" find a measure of relief in the new perspectives provided by Kemal Tahir, Yavuz Aslan, and Andrew Mango, which I have added to the book. It is for this reason that I cannot allow the documents and interpretations in *A Strange Woman* to simply remain as is but instead add new interpretations to subsequent editions. To do otherwise would be considered biased, and such behavior is the archenemy of the novelist.

The situation at hand is due to the fact that previous

generations, who must have had a fuller grasp of this matter than I, almost never addressed it. If only those in Mustafa Kemal's close sphere (Halide Edip, Yakup Kadri Karamosmaoğlu, etc.) had given witness at the time. But the "M. Suphi Incident" has not, to my knowledge, been touched upon in the works of these authors or those who came after: Orhan Kemal, Kemal Tahir, Yaşar Kemal, Aziz Nesin, Rıfat Ilgaz, Çetin Altan, or even in the written works of A. İlhan, who also took a keen interest in the matter. Perhaps it is only now that we are getting close to the truth? For any novelist with half a mind would not dare to write about a historical incident which they did not know well. And mine should be viewed as a kind of whispering acrobatics, undertaken as such so as not to weaken the novel; a call to the idée fixe of "Who killed Suphi?" which has its hooks in Captain Ahmet, too; or an attempt to learn and, together with the society to which it belongs, sate this curiosity.

On the other hand, I would have it known, no matter how meticulous I might be in my research and despite my intention to leave the reader with only the best, I am afraid that, at this rate, *A Strange Woman* will be consigned to oblivion among the countless documents about Mustafa Suphi bound to accumulate over the years!

Leylâ Erbil
(June 2001, Teşvikiye)

PREFACE TO
THE SEVENTH EDITION

I did not find any new documentation to add to this, the seventh edition of *A Strange Woman*, printed in 2005. I apologize to my readers if I have missed anything.

Leylâ Erbil
(2005, Teşvikiye)

PREFACE TO
THE EIGHTH EDITION

I did not find any new documentation to add to this, the eighth edition of *A Strange Woman*, printed in 2011. I apologize to my readers if I have missed anything.

Leylâ Erbil
(2011, Teşvikiye)

THE DAUGHTER

diary '50–'52

Today, Bedri took me and Meral to Lambo's, a small, pleasant tavern near the Beyoğlu Fish Market. All the poets, painters, and journalists go there. Bedri had a poem published in *Varlık*, so he invited us to celebrate, and we drank wine. Without their parents or my parents knowing, of course. If they heard about it, all hell would break loose.

* * *

My mother was on a rampage again today. My father's been fired, she carried on endlessly about it. "He crosses swords with the bosses, talks back to them, as if there's some mansion waiting for us on one of the islands, why make a fuss about law and justice, you'd be better off if you'd just keep your big mouth shut." So I asked, "What do you expect him to do, Mother, let them walk all over him because they're the bosses?" She scolded me, "You keep out of this. You're two of a kind anyway, nothing but hot air for brains." If my father had heard her, he'd have thrown the book at her, but never mind! . .

Meral and I skipped the last lecture and went to Lambo's instead. We met a poet and a short-story writer. They were very nice. I'd like to read my poems to one of them, but I'm too shy. Meral asked me why I don't show my poems to Bedri. She doesn't know her brother's been coming on to me for some time now. I don't much care for him.

Today I told Monsieur Lambo that I'd like to have someone read my poems, and he introduced me right away to a man drinking at the bar. I hadn't realized the man was *Him*. My heart leapt into my throat, I pretended I didn't have the poems with me. We're going to meet tomorrow, at a place called Çardaş in Tünel, and he'll read my poems. That is, if I don't choke on my excitement before then.

Çardaş is a long, dark corridor of a place. A vast, frightening darkness. I couldn't see him at first. A white figure rose and waved from somewhere at the far end. We sat down facing each other and began a halting conversation. He seemed bored or embarassed, and his demeanor infected me, too. I wished a thousand times over that I hadn't come. Suddenly he said, "Well then, chief, let's hear what you've got—go on, read!" His rudeness upset me, and so I struggled through one of my poems, the one that ends with these rather beautiful lines: "Who are they that drive us underground / while the skies are deepest blue, brothers, and our faces so pale." "Are you a worker somewhere?" he asked, dead serious. I couldn't tell if he was making fun of me. I told him, "No, but I have relatives who are." He was silent. Then I read from my "Sonnet of Fallen Girls": "Shall it be always with tears in their eyes that our girls are not sent off to war?" He scratched his nose. "So you want to go to war?" was his response this time. I explained that "war" was used here in a very broad sense; this poem expressed the thought that so long as women were kept from engaging in battles of any sort, they'd end up as an a kind of "army of fallen girls." It was odd that he hadn't gotten the point. To finish, I read my poem "Blood," about the day I got my first period, meant to express the panic that seized me at the time:

> Is this the heel of mighty Achilles
> pierced in my very bed,
> Or some great gaping wound
> where eagles have collided in the sky?
> Ceaseless, the blood
> the pain that settles on her lungs
> drowning eyes, the sea, wrists
> drowning the sea shackled in chains
> drowning drowning ceaselessly.

"What blood is this, I'm not quite with you?" he asked, narrowing his eyes. I'd made that part sound abstract so that it would be difficult to understand. I couldn't tell him the truth, of course, so I said, "I was trying to symbolize the dread of war." "Well done, that's a fine job you've done, but you're a little too young to be a poetess. Let these sit for a few months, then read them over again. I'll bring you some books tomorrow, to Lambo's, read those, too." He was being polite, but he obviously hadn't liked my poems. He was probably laughing to himself the whole time. "Keep on writing, write and then write some more, then put it aside, but never stop writing." Now I was bereft of any hope for my poetry, my sole refuge, my lone consolation. What's the point of living after this, I might as well just die.

I went to Lambo's and picked up the books. He wasn't there. They're all books I've already read! I'm so dreadfully unhappy! . .

* * *

My father got a new job.

* * *

Meral and I went to Lambo's today and met:

an actor just out of prison;

a poet just out of prison;

an architect just out of prison;

a new short-story writer and a new journalist who've never been to prison.

The poet, Halit, and architect, Necat, got up when we were leaving and accompanied us to the bus stop. They were both very nice. We're going to meet them at Degustasyon tomorrow. Meral's crazy about Necat. I have to admit I fancy Halit. He has to go back to his village, to exile, in a week.

* * *

When Meral and Necat went off to a painting exhibition today, Halit and I were left alone at Degustasyon. I suddenly felt a strange fear creep into me. After a while, though, Halit had wiped my fear away. He's a very honest guy. I was a bit late getting home, but my mother didn't notice.

* * *

My mother was crying again today. Aunt Hamdiye came and told her: "They sayin' 'bout you, 'That stranger come an' dried up Hasan's line a'right, couldn't give the man a son.'"

* * *

I met up with Halit again today, at Çardaş this time. He told me about the tortures he'd endured in prison. He described even the most terrible things in a light, mocking way, as though they'd happened to someone else. What an odd guy. For instance, he told me about how they put him through bastinado. He doubled over in laughter the whole time he told me about it . . . And about how they took turns kicking him, how he kicked back at them and spat at one, and how the policeman he'd spat at twisted his balls. It gave me goose bumps. He just laughs; he claims none of it is the police's fault, that that's how they were trained, that they were only doing their duty. Is it some kind of feat, not to let feelings of revenge overtake you in the face of injustice?

* * *

Halit came to the university today, we left and went to Lambo's together. One time the door opened halfway, and *He* seemed about to come in but then saw us and left without a greeting. What an odd man.

Today's the last day. Halit and I met at Degustasyon. I don't know how it happened, but all of a sudden I was confiding in him. My head spun as I talked and talked and talked. About even the most private things, just like when Meral and I tell each other about our problems: my mother's tyranny, how we get on each other's nerves, that I'm some kind of prisoner, the religious pressures she puts on me, the pain I suffer, and even that I've thought of killing myself if I can't get my freedom. That I might run away from home, how nobody understands me, all about my only friend, Meral, and how I took refuge in poetry, that it was the only thing that kept me alive. Something happened to me, I just kept going on and on, I felt more miserable than ever, and I began to cry. He wiped my tears with his handkerchief, as if I were his child. At that I really lost my head and did something that disgusts me now when I recall it: I kissed the hands that were wiping my tears. His fingers smelled of bitter tobacco. I'm shocked at myself that I could do such a thing. Actually, I think I confused the torment he'd endured with my own, it was as though what had happened to him was because of me, and I atoned for it a bit. He was composed as he waited for me to calm down, and then he explained that all suffering was due to the political situation of Turkey, and of the world in general. I thought I understood what he meant, but it still seemed odd to me that he always inserted his mind, like a sharp knife, even into the most delicate moments, like this one. Especially since knowing or understanding does not free you from these predicaments! If I can be happy only once I'm free and the world insists on denying me my freedom, then I simply will never be able to be happy . . . Maybe you can withstand this world if there's someone to share your unhappiness with, maybe if Halit were to stay here, I'd have more strength to withstand it, but he's leaving tomorrow . . . "You're as dear to me as my sisters, come see us anytime you want, whatever we have is yours . . ." He invited me out of the generosity of his heart, he has nothing to share but poverty and hopelessness, I know, yet how happy his existence has made me . . . I broke down completely as he spoke. This time he took my hands in his, turning up my palms and kissing them. There was a long long long silence. When the moment to part came, our eyes were fixed on the grubby tablecloth. From time to time I glanced at some ashes stuck on a piece of white cheese. We lit our last cigarettes. We both knew they were the last. He scribbled

something on the back of a package of Yenice cigarettes and
handed it to me:

> My wounded shattered singing heart
> your eyes the earth and gentle hope
> that is all, my beloved.

Did we love each other, I wonder? Was this what they call
love? If so, it's a little funny, isn't it?

* * *

After bathing today, I put some curlers in my hair. I settled
into the green armchair by the stove. I filed my nails. Father
wasn't back yet. Mother sat down on the edge of the old sofa,
facing me. She was picking some lentils clean. At one point
she stepped out, then returned to the same corner of the sofa
and lit a cigarette. I could feel the storm approaching. She
began with the godless. The tortures in hell awaiting liars. The
wrath meted out to those who don't cover themselves properly. "Why do you wear a hat, then?" I asked. "Your father,"
she snapped, "it's because of your father. May Allah not hold it
a sin, he forced me to wear one. My sins lie on his head." I listened quite a while, without a word. If only she'd leave, I could
go to my room and get back to reading Gorky's "Konovalov."
I've only got a few pages left. I want to absorb it all. I must have
read it ten times. Some passages I already know by heart. She
got up and walked to the door. I lifted my head and watched

her grip the handle. Then suddenly she turned around and asked whether I'd observed the ritual of total ablution during my bath. It was obvious there'd be trouble if I didn't respond. "Yes, I did," I answered, not looking at her. "I don't believe you," she said, planting herself firmly in front of the door, "I don't trust you one bit, your eyes are deceitful. You're capable of anything, anything. You have absolutely no character, you lead a double life. I don't know what exactly, but I can sense that you're keeping something from us. Know that I follow Allah's will. You have to teach your children right from wrong, that's my duty. You can do what you like in secret. But what's done secretly in this world is revealed in the next, don't you forget it. And we'll have to face each other there, too. If you've lied to us, if you've done things in secret, snakes and centipedes will devour you in the next world . . ." "I got the message," I said as I tried to get away. "What's that, young lady, didn't care for my advice?" she said, blocking the door. "I have to study for my lessons," I said. "Aren't these lessons? These are Allah's own lessons, now get out of my face, and to hell with your lessons," she said and then slapped me. I ran to my room, crying. I'm going to read "Konovalov" now.

* * *

I met a guy named Halûk today. He's studying history. He was very forthright, he didn't eye me at all the whole time we spoke. I felt comfortable with him. He's obviously poor, his clothes were falling apart.

LEYLÂ ERBİL

* * *

Halûk was wandering the hallway in the same gray jacket, check-
ered shirt, and unsightly shoes. We were both an hour early for
class. We went to the cafeteria. He noticed I was carrying a book
by Gorky and took an interest. "He's good," he said, as if he knew
a thing or two. We talked. He lives in Kadiköy. Says he doesn't
have a home of his own, that he's from Cyprus, and that he's staying with a rich relative. "Or rather, in an outbuilding," he said,
"I'm a night watchman of sorts." He had a pile of books under
his arm. He gave me some translations by Kerim Sadi to read.

* * *

Kevser, Ayten, Şeref, Sadi, and I went to a tea at the medical
school. I told my mother I had a language seminar. Ayten has no
father, her mother's a widow, a civil servant somewhere. Ayten
says I should go for Sadi. "But why?" I asked, and she said, "Why
not, he's good-looking." How odd, the way Ayten always insists
on flirting with someone. And she's the kind of girl who, if someone falls for her, she immediately reciprocates, doesn't matter
who. She's not choosy at all. The tea was a dull affair. Just a lot of
boys and girls dancing together. What nonsense.

* * *

Halûk introduced me to one of his friends today. He called him
Ömer Ağbi. We talked about literature for a while. Neither of

them like Tolstoy. Between them they massacred the great man. The conversation then turned to Nâzim Hikmet. Ömer likes his honesty, his behavior better than his poetry. Strange fellow, this Ömer. "Call me Ömer Ağbi, sister," he told me. "All right," I said. I think he's from the East. Like my Halit.

* * *

Aunt Havva's oldest daughter, Neriman, just had a son. Her husband's been transferred to Ankara, they're off tomorrow. She came to say goodbye and kiss my mother's hand. Mother talked about Neriman all evening, telling me what a girl she is, how she's university-educated yet remains devout. How she fasts during the holy month, and helps her mother around the house. And she keeps every single hair on her head covered.

* * *

I'm not ever going to dance again. Or go to teas. You go out to the dance floor to dance, then go back to your seat. For some time now, on my way back to my seat from the dance floor, I've felt strange, embarrassed, regretful. I'm not sure what it means, but it's disgusting, that walk back from the dance floor. The other girls kept smirking all the way back to their seats, every time.

* * *

The girls insisted I go to the engineers' tea. At home, I said I was going to a birthday party for Ayten. For some reason, my mother likes Ayten: "You can tell just from looking at her that she's a good, honest girl . . ." I didn't dance, just watched the others return from the dance floor to their seats. Kevser and Şeref danced cheek to cheek. Leaning their heads against each other. Well apart below the waist. Protecting their honor that way, I suppose. Kevser had painted her cheeks the color of a toffee apple. A guy named Ahmet—he said he was a friend of Şeref's—came over to invite me to dance. I said no. He asked me why, and I explained. He told me I was "real nice," and asked me what I was into. I told him "poetry" and right away he started spouting off. His demeanor suggested, "You name the goods, and I'll deliver." He informed me that Nâzım Hikmet would be a good poet if he weren't so politically driven in his art. He said he liked Ziya Osman Saba very much, and that he didn't care for Orhan Veli at all. Whatever that's supposed to mean. I suddenly realized that he was making it all up then and there, but I refrained from telling him so to his face. I just kept silent. After a while he stopped talking, too. He'd depleted his repertoire. He said he'd come by the department to see me. Really, and just what does he think I'd do if he did!

Told Halûk about yesterday's tea and Ahmet. We had a good laugh. I've just begun Freud's *Totem and Taboo*. "Don't waste your time," he told me. If I wanted to educate myself properly, there were other books I should read first. He's going to bring me some next time, on the condition I read and return them within one week. They're forbidden books, apparently. Halûk's a nice guy but difficult to understand. He seems convinced that all the professors are stupid, brainwashed charlatans. "You'll realize it, too, one day," he added.

In between classes, Şeref, Kevser, and I were sitting in the cafeteria together. Out of the blue, Ahmet showed up. He wore a sickly yellow pullover and had his hair combed back. He sat down, I didn't speak to him at all, the whole atmosphere at the table became weird. When he and Şeref went to leave, he squeezed my hand so hard I yelled out, "Ouch!" The others were startled. Şeref gave Ahmet a nasty look.

* * *

Halûk arrived with a bag full of books today. He handed it to me. "Don't give or show them to anybody, just read them yourself, and keep them hidden," he warned.

Kevser brings me daily news of Ahmet. Says he's been keeping Şeref up all night back in their dorm ever since that day at the cafeteria. Seems he's madly in love with me. Supposedly he can't concentrate on his classes because of me. He spends all day playing cards in the coffeehouses of Sultanahmet, all because of his passion for me. "How pathetic," I told Kevser. She was put out. She and Şeref thought they were going to sell me on the idea of a romance with that fool.

* * *

I'm reading the books Halûk gave me. There were also some
handwritten announcements and assorted tracts in the bag.
I burned the lot. Now I'm reading G. Deville's *Capital*. The
translator is Haydar Rıfat. He dedicated it to "Sir Şekerzade
Edip İzzet." What romantic men, these old translators.

* * *

I got a letter from Halit. He wrote a long poem about me. A
really beautiful poem, actually. I wrote him back this evening.
About life here, things that have happened to me, everything.
I sent him my latest poems. But right now I'm more interested
in the situations I'm in, and people, than in writing poetry. The
poems I sent him aren't very good, I know.

* * *

They've arrested Halûk and a few others with him. I'm terribly
upset. What's going to happen now!

* * *

As soon as I got home, I hid Halûk's books. In case they come to
search for them. I wonder why he was arrested. It's not like the
poor guy did anything wrong. I don't feel like seeing anyone at all.
I'll make up some story to tell my mother and stay at home today.
Should I try to visit Halûk? What sort of a place is prison anyway?
He's at the one in Sultanahmet. What will they do to the boy!

I had a dream tonight, in black-and-white.

I'm looking at a picture. A picture painted a long time ago. What the paint is made of, who made it, or how isn't clear. It's filled with people on a white background. People drawn in black lines. I take the picture and go out into the street, I start walking down this long, narrow street when suddenly Bedri appears, and I show him the picture, and we walk together. The street is so long and so narrow that the light at the end of it shines like the moon. Above us is a long, thin strip of sky. Suddenly the picture rises up into the air until it covers the entire sky. These people made of soot fill the sky, like stickers. The white background of the picture is replaced by the faded blue of the sky. Bedri runs off shouting, "People, people!" Then he finds an open door and slips inside to hide. I run after him, but he shuts the door in my face. There's no one in the street except me and a few children. The children are in tears, dashing about, then they start running toward me. "Don't be afraid!" I tell them, but then I, too, begin to shout "Mommy! Mommy!" and weep along with them. The stickers begin falling from the sky and raining down upon us. They're falling down toward the rooftops. It's getting dark, it reeks of soot and burning everywhere. My mother appears out of the moon-shaped light at the end of the street, with a white chamber pot in her hand. "Don't be afraid, I'm coming," she shouts. The people made of soot are falling down left and right, onto the earth, between the stones. One lands on my right thigh and sticks to it. I look and see that it's Bedri. My mother places the pot under me and urges, "Repent, repent, ask for God's forgiveness. You've sinned, tell me what you've done, are you still a virgin?" "Mother dear, I haven't done anything wrong!" I say. I feel a breeze, it comes nearer and nearer, blows all the soot away, the children give cries of joy. The sticker of Bedri that was stuck to my leg disappears. The chamber pot grows the length of the street, all the way to the end, and is filled with flags, tiny flags of every nation. The children run up and scramble to grab them. My mother says, "You take one, too, I want to see which one you'll choose." I grab the one nearest me, I look and see that it's a plain black-and-white flag. I wake up. It's 5:00 AM as I write this in my diary. I'm going to go to Sultanahmet to see Halûk.

* * *

Today Meral and I went to the movies. When I took my ticket from the man at the counter, I told him, "Merci," and he replied, "Up yours."

* * *

I went to see Halûk. He was really pleased. He didn't think I'd come. And he was surprised. He told me that he and the others had been arrested for underground activities. And so now he has to serve out the rest of his sentence. "I already knew it would happen, I've got another five months in here," he said. He asked for a cigarette, I didn't have any, I gave him two and a half liras so he could have a pack bought for him. How curly his eyelashes are. You can hardly see his eyes for his lashes. His face was sectioned by the grid of the iron bars; sometimes one eye and a bit of forehead were framed in a square, sometimes his nose or his chin. His nose is small and bends slightly to the left. He was unshaven, his beard sparse and curly. His teeth are yellow as can be. I bet he never brushes them. He kind of looks Jewish. I told him I'd begun to read *Capital* but found it a tough nut to crack. He gave me the names of other books I should read first. He made me memorize a message for Ömer Ağabey. I was to tell him, "The white crow needs food." He told me Ömer Ağabey can't come around. I'm to go and find him in Cibali. Halûk had me memorize his address. He told me whatever I did, not to write it down anywhere. He added that he "personally" trusted me, but that he couldn't explain any more right now. "We'll probably be closer friends in the future," he said. He then asked me to think hard before deciding whether to do what he'd asked. "Do it only if you're not afraid, fear is no disgrace, but once you begin, you can't stop halfway, you can't reveal what I've told you, even if they try to kill you, only Ömer Ağbi can hear it," he told me. We were both silent after that. Then he repeated, "Think hard, if you decide not to go ahead, then forget what I've told you and don't come here again, don't greet me if you see me anywhere, it will be as though we've never met." I laughed. "You don't know me at all," I said. He laughed, too. I left and went back home. He truly doesn't know me. I'd give my life for people like him. I don't know why, but my feelings propel me to such people. I think they're like me. I believe they are defying evil.

* * *

I went to Cibali today. I found Ömer Ağabey's place like I'd put it there myself. Two little basement rooms on a narrow street. The sign over the door says "Electrician." The part where he lives is on the other side of a glass partition. He has a table and three chairs. Through the glass, you can see the workers on the other side. He probably wants to be able to keep an eye on them so they don't goof off, there were two young boys in overalls at work there. When he saw me, Ömer Ağabey leapt to his feet and called out, "Sister, come here!" He threw his arms around me and thumped my back a few times. No one had ever hugged me so warmly. I was very moved. I understood that I was made for this, that I could follow these people anywhere, eyes closed. He was drinking linden tea. He'd already had a few sips, I think, but handed me the glass. "You drink it, I'll order another for myself," he said. "I saw Halûk," I declared. "Tell me about it, sister." He didn't ask if there was a message for him, just looked at me. I waited a little. He still didn't ask. He wasn't going to. "The white crow needs food," I said. "The cheeky fellow!" he immediately exclaimed. Then, "Long may you live, sister! Is that all?" "That's all," I said. "Done," he declared. "Off you go now, this isn't the safest place to be, wouldn't want you to get into any trouble." He sent me away without even letting me finish my linden tea, had me take a shorter route than the one I'd come by. I looked back from the top of the garden steps and saw that he'd pulled on his workman's cap and was about to leave. What an exciting day it's been. This is exactly how I want every one of my days to be.

* * *

I went to see Halûk again. I gave him five liras. I told him what had happened. "Okay, thank you," was all he said. Then I suddenly started telling him about Halit. "We were friends," he said, "he's a good guy." He seemed a bit put off, though. He didn't say anything else. On my way out, he told me, "You'd better not come again. I'm afraid you might get into trouble because of us." "Oh, come on," I said with a laugh.

* * *

Meral's family have bought a house in Pendik and moved there. "Bedri's in love with you, he keeps asking about you," she told me.

I'm at home today. I told my mother I had to prepare for the winter prelims. She looked hard at me but asked no questions. I wrote Halit a long letter. I mentioned Halûk. Just wrote that I'd met him and that he was now serving his last few months in prison. I didn't say anything about him knowing Halit. Am curious to know what Halit will say. I did a lot of thinking today. Mostly about Halûk. Who is he, what is he? Why do I have such trust in him and his friends, and them alone? It's not just trust, though, more like respect. Who am I, what am I doing, and what are they doing? "The white crow needs food." What is this all about, why doesn't he tell me? Whatever would I do if my mother and father heard about it? Do these people have any ties with Moscow, I wonder? But that's impossible. The Moscow connection is surely just something the police made up. Who are they? . . Well, it doesn't matter who they are. I'm going to do what I feel is right. I'm going to be one of them. Anything that will help us be different from the older generations, from our mothers.

* * *

Kevser and I went to the movies. We saw *Viva Zapata!*, it was wonderful. Kevser is a strange girl. She's modest and conceited at the same time. She's from Izmir. Her father owns a textile factory there. She told me all about her views on life. If she bags Şeref, she's going to marry him and settle in Izmir. Her father's already had a house built for her in Karşıyaka. The deed's in her name, because she has a stepmother. Şeref will be given a job in her father's firm so that the stepmother doesn't try any tricks. "No way we're letting that woman get hold of any money, any property," she said. I was astonished, maybe if I'd been brought up under the same circumstances, I'd know, too, which side my bread was buttered on. After the movie, we dropped in at Lambo's. She really liked it. But she warned me, "Don't you dare tell Şeref." I agreed. No letter from Halit.

* * *

This morning, I was about to walk into school when a youngish man stopped me in my tracks. A policeman. I said I had no business with the police. "You will for about an hour, now please come with me," he said. There was no escape, the man was determined to make me go with him. I have no idea how to act in such a situation—how stupid of me not to have found out. There must be a certain way of talking with a policeman, of following him. Anyway, we began walking together. *Go on now,* I said to myself, *don't be scared, what have you done, you've taken a first step toward destroying the rotten social order, that's what. You can do it, go on, forward march, left-right, left-right. Even if they try to kill you, you won't talk, even if they try to kill you . . .* The man wore an enormous black felt hat like a blind man's, and he walked without saying a word. Who knows what my mother would say if she saw me like this. I'm not afraid of the police, but I am afraid of her, of home, if they hear about it. We went into a building. We went up the stairs, into a room. A rosy-cheeked man, forty-five, fifty years old, was sitting behind a desk. "I've brought her, sir," my escort said and then left. Once we were alone, the man at the desk took a good long look at me. "You called for me, might I know the reason?" I asked. I was sweating from the rushed journey there. He asked my name, what school I went to, my mother's and father's names, and wrote it all down. Then he stood up and said, "Aren't you ashamed of yourself?" "Why should I be ashamed?" I asked. "Tell me what went on between you and that dog Salih?" "I don't know anyone named Salih," I answered. He said they knew that I'd been to see Ömer Ağabey. His real name is Salih. "Go on, tell me," he said. I told him I had nothing to tell, that I knew Halûk, that he was my friend, that when he was in jail I'd simply done my duty as a human being. The man walked right up to me, "You idiot," he said, looking the idiot himself. "We weren't born yesterday, who the hell do you think you're fooling, I'll rip that pig face of yours to shreds . . ." He piled on the threats, trying to frighten me. They came in such profusion that after a while I simply didn't hear what he was saying, I was just trying to calculate what he could really do. I didn't worry so much about being beaten up, but I thought, *Suppose he throws me down and does something beastly to me. Suppose that precious bit of membrane which my mother values so highly is torn apart by a policeman. And in a setting like this to boot.* It was a bare wooden floor, and I thought to myself, *If I make it out of here in one piece, the first thing I'll do is find a sensible guy to rid me of this stupid thing, it's such a nasty business. Maybe Ahmet.* Stifling a laugh, I looked at the man, he was still rambling on, foaming at the mouth. There was something affected about his manner, a sort of swagger. Then a slap stung my face. I screamed, startling even myself. The man stepped back. It hadn't really hurt much, but I hadn't expected it. "You've no right to do this," I shouted. "You idiot," he grinned. The door opened, and another youngish man stepped in. My guy promptly stood at attention. The new man began to talk at once, asking me my name as he sat down. "Young lady, my advice to you is that you focus on your studies and not get mixed up in anything else. I am a law graduate, and I have a lot of experience in these matters." "In that case," I replied, showing him my bloody tooth, "you know that people shouldn't be beaten up for no reason! I'm holding you responsible." He pretended to give the other man, who was still standing, an angry look. "Keep away from the Communists, and don't end up here again, they can get you into enough trouble to destroy both you and your family." He stood up and said goodbye. As soon as I was back on the street, I took out my compact and had a look, my lip was swollen, a little blood trickled from my tooth, and half my cheek near the corner of my mouth was red. Those asses, those sons of bitches, those bastards. On my way back to the university, I went through all the swear words I knew. I stopped by the cafeteria, but there was nobody there. I walked upstairs to Tanpınar's lecture. He's been talking about Yahya Kemal's poetry for several classes now.

> *Last night your revels were ceaselessly gay,*
> *The sound of lutes floated across the bay,*
> *At dawn, when songs grew dim and waters gray,*
> *That was my caïque, oh beloved, drifting by.*

So your caïque was drifting by, so what? Now she's supposed to love you back, is that it? Whose property was that caïque, anyway? Did Yahya Kemal have his own caïque? If so, how much did he pay for it? How did he earn the money? Who was rowing it? What was his beloved like? Whose daughter was she, was she rich, was she beautiful?

* * *

A letter from Halit. He knows Halûk very well. They were interrogated at the same time. "Stay away from him," he writes.

45

He'll tell me all about Halûk when he sees me. Plus plans for escape, again, and a poem.

* * *

Everybody keeps looking at everybody else. Everywhere. When you're sitting, when you're at your desk, in the class-room, with a lecturer, with your friends, they look at you, and you look at them. What goes on inside of them? Meral brought me a letter from Bedri today. When she came to my house. He just repeats what he's been saying for the last three years: "Let's talk." About what! Meral is very happy, she runs to Necat after classes, they meet every day. They're enough for each other. I don't think I could ever be that kind of girl.

* * *

Kevser, Ayten, and I had a heart-to-heart. Kevser looked chic, as usual. What a lot of money she must spend on clothes—I get maybe two pairs of shoes a year, she has a slew of them, in every style and color. Şeref is in his last year at law school, they're to get engaged as soon as he graduates. Şeref's father is a minor civil servant. He's not going to practice law, though, he's going to work with Kevser's father. And Kevser's going to quit university at the end of the year. "If I quit now, I won't be able to see Şeref, and if he's left alone, somebody else might try to snatch him." Ayten has yet another new boyfriend, a medi-cal student, they met at a tea.

* * *

I'm reading *Crime and Punishment*. Fantastic characters. Bedri suddenly appeared today; he insisted we sit and have a chat. I refused. The guy's eyes are like decapitated wasps, they hover around me, stingers out. But he does have that thing they call sex appeal! Kevser didn't come to class today. Şeref came by, went a little crazy when he found she wasn't there.

* * *

Kevser skipped class again. Şeref waited and waited for her, then finally left. I went to Kevser's dorm. Seems she has pneumonia and went to her aunt's house in Şişli. I went straight there to see her. Her father'd been sent for, too. She gave me a letter for Şeref.

* * *

Ayten and I went to the movies after class today. A film about Chopin's life was playing. I thought George Sand was fantastic. What a woman! Once again my mother greeted me with insults. I told her I'd been in a linguistics class. She didn't fall for it. "That place isn't a university, it's a brothel," she kept saying. When it was time for father's return, she complained of a headache and went to bed. What an odd woman, when she's certain of a transgression of mine, she doesn't tell my father, she keeps it to herself. I waited for him to scold me, but nothing. She must not have told him about me being late. My father's so stupid, he really thought she was sick and ran around in circles all night. He took her temperature, felt her pulse, cooked her supper and took it to her in bed. Yet there's absolutely nothing the matter with her, I'm sure of it. Just as I suspected, no temperature. It's as if she wants to tell me that I've made her sick with my behavior, all the while, she's using my father. After supper, I called up to Mother and she told me to make them coffee. I did, washed the dishes, too. Then I retreated into *Crime and Punishment*. Father leaves tomorrow.

* * *

Crime and Punishment.

* * *

My mother took my copy of *Crime and Punishment* and tossed it into the stove. "I'm going to tell your father," she threatened. "If you think I'll keep all your filth from him, you're wrong. I'm going to tell him that you lie to me, telling me that you're studying when you're reading novels . . ." I snapped back, "Tell him whatever you want." Ugh, I've had enough! . .

* * *

Today was horrible:
    Şeref came to school today. He asked about Kevser. I told

him. "She's better now, though," I said. "She'll come see you as soon as she's up and about, she sent you this letter." He took the letter. "Whatever," he said, shoving the letter into his pocket. We were in the garden. Suddenly, right then and there, he declared his love for me. "After I hadn't seen Kevser for a few days, I realized it, this terrible truth," he said. I asked him what he hoped to gain by telling me this. "I wasn't going to tell you, but I couldn't help myself, I don't expect anything of you." "Well, let's just agree, then, that you've said nothing, and I've heard nothing," I said. "I know I shouldn't have told you, but if I hadn't, I would've gone crazy," he said with a long face. I couldn't help but feel curious, how much of this was he making up? Or was he sincere? "Well, what is it you love about me?" I asked. "What's it to you, why are you asking, I'm not asking you to love me back," he replied, letting the words out slowly. I liked that. It was something different, and it sparked my interest. Relenting a little, I said, "If you like, I can cut classes for the rest of the day and we can talk it over." I don't know why, I took him to Lambo's. We drank some wine. He didn't speak, he seemed to be sulking, or embarrassed. "Let's go to somewhere else," he said. We shared the bill. We went to a café directly opposite Lambo's. As soon as we sat down, he began: "I know it's impossible, and probably even immoral, but what can I do, I've come to realize that I love you, not her. For days now I've been showing up just to get a glimpse of you. I'm simply not interested in Kevser at all . . ." I still kept wondering what it was about me that attracted him. What could it be? He didn't even mention me but kept going on about Kevser and himself.

And he kept drinking wine, and then he started giving me these piercing looks, narrowing his eyes. It was so weird. After all this time, almost a year, when we've been together so often as just friends, why would he change like this? Guilt suddenly swept over me, and I longed to get away. Just then, Şeref went to the restroom. When he sat down again, I noticed the sheets of paper hanging from his pocket, with Kevser's handwriting on them. I was annoyed that he'd read the letter secretly in the restroom. But I tried not to show it. Could he be so deceitful? What was the point of all this? I'd never shown any interest in him or given him any encouragement. Or was this some kind of ploy to try and make me jealous? Even in that case, it only revealed his utter lack of character. "Well, Casanova, out with it, why are you doing this?" I said, he didn't get it. He hadn't done it on purpose. "Don't talk like that, I respect you," he said. "Well, why do you respect me, what is it you love about me, and why?" He thought he had me hooked, and he rattled off, "Everything about you: your sincerity, your naturalness, your honesty, your body, you're so beautiful, you're not like the others. Kevser hasn't got anything that you do . . ." "Right," I began, "I've listened to you, now what would you like me to do? I understand, I believe you. You don't love Kevser, you love me, so what's going to happen now?" "Nothing!" he said. "Nothing. I just wanted to tell you." "Is that so!" I said. He fell silent. Even when drunk, he was still calculating. He thought for sure I'd fall for it, and so he was careful not to let anything slip, not to make any vague promises. What filthy cunning! If everything went according to his plan, when Kevser returned the next day, he'd pick up where he left off, become the groom who moves in with his rich in-laws, all the while having his little affair with me on the side. I decided to teach him a lesson. "I want to tell you about me and my feelings for you," I said, deepening my voice to fit the scene of a clandestine love affair. "I've known you for a year now," I continued. He listened, lips parted in eager anticipation. "But I've never liked you, never, at all. I'm fond of Kevser, and so I've had to put up with seeing you. But first, what I look for in a friend, let alone a lover, is integrity, and you possess not one iota of it." I told him, "Don't interrupt me. You could've read Kevser's letter in front of me, you know—or did you think I'd be jealous?" He flushed, and plunged his hand into his pocket. I let out a long laugh, just to make him angry. He stood up. "You're going to pay your share of the bill," I declared, "and then take your leave like a man!" He tossed five liras onto the table and stormed off. The piece of shit!

* * *

Ran into Bedri today. He said if I refused to speak to him, he'd kill himself. His eyes were on my breasts the whole time he spoke, like a caveman or something. He was breathing hard, and, as he's quite a bit taller than me, his breath ruffled the hair on top of my head. I told him I'd talk to him some other day, just so he'd let me go. Back home, I brushed my hair. It was really tangled on top. What a strange thing to happen, so creepy.

* * *

Ayten and I have planned a trick on Bedri. The three of us will go out together. I'll find some excuse to leave the two of them alone. Ayten will drink with him and lead him on. Then we'll know whether he's really in love with me. If he isn't, then this business will be over and I'll be free. I don't particularly like him, but, of course, if he passes the test, I'll think more highly of him. I might even make him a gift of this little membrane of mine. He's perfectly cut out for the job, to be honest.

* * *

Kevser is back. I went up to her when I saw her in the cafeteria. Can you believe that vile girl turned and greeted me with, "So, you're waiting for Şeref again, are you?" I was stunned. I'm surprised I didn't faint. Or burst into tears. Though I felt like doing all of it, I managed to hold myself together. "If you love him so much, I'll just take my leave so you can have him all to yourself," she said. The dirty rotten creatures! I struggled to keep my composure. I articulated every word of my response clearly, as if I couldn't care less. "He's not telling the truth, he lied to you." "Aren't there enough men for you that you have to go and seduce your friends' lovers?" she asked. "Don't be impertinent," I said . . . She wasn't even listening, her eyes flashed with anger, so much blood had rushed to her head I thought she might drown in it. That scion of a textile empire. So the tale is that I'm madly in love with Şeref, and he pitied me and agreed to meet just once, to placate me, and I raised hell because I saw him reading Kevser's letter!.. "Look," I told her, "he's deceiving you. The moment he saw me in the garden, he burst out that he was in love with me, not you, I wouldn't give a lowly creature like him the time of day." She burst out in a rattling laugh; she must have learned it from her stepmother! She was always going on about how the woman bewitched her father with her laughter. "If he has an ounce of decency in him, then he should confront me himself," I told her. "As if everyone doesn't already know what kind of girl you are," she said, "to think Şeref would declare his love for you, the nerve, when you'd have settled for the likes of that orangutan Halûk long ago, but no, you're out to break us up." There was nothing more to say. All that remained was for us to get into a catfight and rip each other's hair out. I walked away. She let out another of her stepmother's guffaws as I left. I'd never dreamed that people, that Şeref and Kevser, could sink so low. The other students in the cafeteria heard everything, how can I ever look them in the face again? I don't know how I got out of there, but next thing I knew, I was at Lambo's. Haydar was there, too. He's a good guy. "There's something the matter, why don't you tell me about it, I'll be glad to help if I can," he said. What could I tell him? Suppose he, too, came to have doubts about my character?.. They've accused me of playing the role I despise most in this world, a role I'm utterly incapable of!.. Those lowlifes—I detest them!..

* * *

I haven't been to lectures for a week. I've been staying at home, studying for exams. Sometimes I say I'm off to school and go to Lambo's instead. And I'm looking for a job, being careful to keep it from my parents, though. Halit's started writing me love letters. But they're really more like literary exercises. I get it. A young man exiled to a gloomy eastern town, of course he's going to fall in love with the first person who comes along. I mean, if it were somebody else, and not me, he'd still be in love. The way he writes, I can tell his nerves are shot. I'm afraid he might try to harm himself. He tried once before, cut his wrists while in prison, I know. There's a strong bond between us . . . I read his letters as if the love he says he feels isn't for me, but for someone else; like I'm reading a novel. I interpret them objectively. I know he hasn't got anyone else, no one to love, to write to. So I write him friendly letters, not making any sexual promises. Halit's so important to me. If he were to hurt me, I'd take it very hard. Sometimes when I turn and look at myself, I find myself so hopeless, so full of despair, so pathetic that my eyes well up. But I have a strength inside of me, I believe that the others are wrong, and that I am right and just. This strength is what keeps me from crumbling. And Halit, as well as Haydar. Meral, too, to a degree. I told Meral about what Şeref and Kevser did, she knows the inside story, she's not speaking to them. I wrote to Halit. "Don't you go anywhere near those bougie bastards, sweetheart," he says, "they'll just upset you; they're incapable of understanding my one and only darling girl." And so with just a few words he keeps me from falling apart.

* * *

Went to school today. I went straight to class. To our English Crone's lesson. Ayten and I were leaving when Bedri stopped us in our tracks. I asked Ayten to wait and had a few words with him. Tomorrow, "but only if we're not alone. I'm bringing Ayten with me," I said. He agreed, we'll see what happens.

* * *

Ha ha ha ha ha . . . It's too funny for words . . . Ha ha ha. It's just too much, too much. I met Bedri at Trianon. With Ayten, too, of course. It's a coffee shop near Galatasaray. On a discreet side street. When Ayten and I walked in and sat down, Bedri didn't even look at her, just started devouring me with his eyes. From time to time he gave me a reproachful glance and seemed about to say something. Then Ayten stood up and undressed. By which I mean she removed her coat. But the way she did it, you'd have thought she was taking everything off. Teasingly, like some strange writhing creature. She wore a fire engine–red pullover with a tight skirt the same color. And a black belt around her waist. The skirt was beyond anything, you couldn't pay someone to wear it. Anyway, the pullover was so tight that her nipples showed. I took a good look and could tell she wasn't wearing a bra. My boy's eyes were now fixed on her, and remained there for the duration. Ayten had painted her lips the same red. She kept licking them and throwing Bedri furtive glances through squinted eyes. Every now and then she gave me a wink. At one point, she expressed surprise at the width of Bedri's shoulders and touched them with her fingers, which she then withdrew as though they'd felt fire, before exclaiming "Wow!" with a shudder, in a strange, low voice. Even I couldn't tell whether she meant what she said or was just carrying out our plan. Bedri, meanwhile, was getting taller and taller. After a while, he shifted his chair so that only Ayten was in his line of vision. And he didn't look at me again, not once. Truth is, I was rather annoyed. At one point Ayten went to the toilet. The way she twisted her waist and shook her bottom as she stood up, even I couldn't take my eyes off her. When we were alone, I turned to look at Bedri. He looked at me, one eyebrow up in the air—what a look—as if to say, "Now you see what I'm made of," that piece of shit third-rate boxer. He's been taking boxing lessons for years at the Community Center in Eminönü. You know, so that if that colonel father of his ever hits him again, he can take him out with a single punch. How right I was not to encourage him all these years. I didn't utter a word until Ayten returned. The trick had worked. As soon as Ayten was back, I said, "Oh, you guys, I just realized: today's Thursday, my mother and I are supposed to go shopping for a pair of shoes, I forgot—you stay, I have to go," and leapt to my feet. I winked at Ayten and she winked back. Bedri didn't even suggest accompanying me. "You go along, darling," Ayten said, "we might as well stay a bit longer." I wonder what happened after. I guess I'll find out tomorrow.

* * *

It was just as I thought. The moment I was gone, Bedri told Ayten he was madly, madly in love with her. About me, he explained, "I thought I was in love with her, but all this time I was really looking for someone like you." He told her he'd been completely swept off his feet. When there were no waiters around, he grabbed her wrist and kissed it so hard he left a mark, I saw it myself. Bit it rather than kissed it, I think. He asked to see her again. Ayten told him she was seeing someone else, and it wouldn't be fair to me, since I was her friend, that sort of thing. "I don't care who you've been seeing, and nothing that's happened to you until now is of any importance," Bedri said. "Well, you know, I've never been into the boy at all myself, so you don't need to worry about hurting my feelings," I told Ayten, "and he's not a bad guy, really." She replied with, "Oh no, dear, I could never" and so forth. The truth is I would've liked for her to have a bit of fun with Bedri and then drop him, but I think she's really into him. She's been looking for a "steady boyfriend" long enough, and he's about as steady as she's going to find. For some reason, I was shaken by a feeling akin to jealousy and disgust as I left her today. After all, Bedri is my childhood friend. To think he's been after me for all these years yet goes and falls for another girl in the space of an hour, unbelievable.

* * *

This morning I saw an ad in the paper, so I went and applied. I got the job, at Mum Han in Karaköy. I'm to answer the office telephone. It's a parallel line. The boss is a young man with glasses. My job is this: the boss and I are to be there every day; I answer the telephone and ask who's calling, while he listens on the other line, and when he hears the name of the person calling, he winks at me if he wants to speak to them, and I hang up, and if he doesn't want to speak to them, I dodge them for the time being, say he's not in, that they should call back in an hour or whatnot. Of course, I'm to sit at a desk directly opposite the boss's, so that I can tell if he's winking or not, and for this job he'll pay me two hundred liras a month to work from nine till five, during which time I'm not to leave at all. We're to eat lunch there together, too, for which he'll deduct thirty liras from my salary. What an utterly odd job. The guy didn't tell me what it is he actually does. He just keeps saying, "People call me." A man whose job is to receive phone calls. And he's rented himself an office exclusively for that purpose.

* * *

Dropped in at Lambo's, there was no letter. There was nobody there, either. After a while M. S. the Poet arrived. He sat down by himself. Lambo has a bad cold, a drop of snot dangled from the red tip of his pointed nose. It made me sick to my stomach. When he's filling a glass of wine, he holds the glass right under his nose. M. S.'s poems are about people, or their anger. The guy's plenty angry himself, and has the weirdest tics. Like he's some kind of cripple or something. He puts on the airs of a great poet in an attempt to impress me. He thinks he's going to dazzle me with his nervous tics, his hard drinking and no eating—though he's got plenty of money—his grandiloquent words, and his endless quoting of French poetry. His latest number is socialist realism. He's constantly dropping the phrase *socialist realism* as if you could be a socialist without being a realist. I haven't come across a single good poem by him so far. Mediocre poetry, the kind of stuff government employees produce. He writes for *Varlık*. There's this saying he loves to repeat: "Like kebab—roasted on swords, roasted on swords they should be!" He's referring to other poets like himself.

We've had all our exams. I passed mine. Whenever I run into Kevser, I get goose bumps. We don't speak at all. The funny thing is, she hasn't told anyone else about what happened between us. Not even Ayten. I sounded Meral out about it, but she says Kevser hasn't mentioned anything. Şeref doesn't come by as often as he used to. If I'd run into him right after what happened, I'd have torn a strip off of him, but now I see the two of them leaving together sometimes, and what I feel isn't anger but a kind of bitter emptiness.

* * *

People, people, people. Now it is only people that interest me. What a treasure trove. My head spins when I meet someone new. Until I find out what kind of person they are, and what they're capable of. People really set my head spinning . . .

* * *

I've read almost all of Dostoyevsky's books, everything that's been published here so far. What a fantastic writer. And how well he understands people. Like with me, people are his main concern, too. I no longer write poetry, it is impossible to squeeze people into poetry, they are simply too vast. That's how I understand poetry, art in general, these days: art is a deep well, full of people.

I saw *Him* today in Pera. Meral and Necat were coming out of an art exhibition. He stopped to talk to Necat and gave me a quick greeting, lasted a split second, just a greeting. I wanted to tell him I'd read his books, to say something, anything, but he didn't give me a chance. As soon as he was done speaking with Necat, he just slipped away. Flew off, you might even say.

* * *

Halûk is out. We ran into each other in the faculty garden. They released him early, even. I ran up to him, put my arms around his neck, and kissed him on both cheeks. He seemed embarrassed. We sat down on a rock in a corner. He thanked me. I told him about everything that had happened—why I hadn't been back to see him, my encounter with the police, etc. "I know," he said. "You did what you were supposed to do." It seems they've arrested Ömer Ağabey now, too. "I didn't tell

the police a thing," I said. "I know," he replied again. He acted
like he didn't quite believe things had happened like I said, as
if I were guilty of something. I felt offended, remained silent.
Then I told him that Ömer Ağabey's real name was Salih. "I
know that, too," he said. I thought he might explain things to
me, tell me what *white crow* meant. But no. I was going to ask
him but then decided against it, thought my curiosity would
come across as simple. "You did what you were supposed to,"
that's all he said. He could have told me more, but he didn't
want to. Whatever *white crow* means, my learning it would be
of no use to the cause. Still, I was hurt by the lack of trust his
actions revealed. He soon got up and scurried off to class, as if
in a hurry. I was left staring after him.

* * *

Necat has split up with Meral. He's married a rich girl and
lives with his in-laws. The girl's mother put up the capital for
him to set up an architecture office. Apparently Necat's saying stuff like, "We've done our share, we've had our fill of poverty and misery, now it's the next generation's turn to carry on
the struggle." Bedri and Ayten are thoroughly in love. They're
sleeping together, Meral tells me. He takes her to a friend's
pied-à-terre. "But I think he's getting bored of her, he's been
asking after you again," she said. "He graduates this year, you
know, he'll be practicing medicine soon. Wouldn't be a bad
thing if you made up." "I'm not angry with him," I told her, "but
that's another matter. Bedri and I could never get along, better

to forget about it." Meral is such a good person. She says what
she means, and she means what she says. We've been going
to Lambo's together again. It's much better when she doesn't
have a boyfriend, she goes along with whatever I want to do. I
can get her to agree to any prank. Apparently there's some gossip about me circulating around the university and among the
Lambo regulars. I kind of like the gossip. Being accused of all
sorts of things that I haven't done. Stupid, ridiculous things.
All this gossip is teaching me about so many different aspects
of people: how surprising they can be, how greedy, how benev-
olent, how dismissive, how selfish. There's nothing they're
not capable of, the lot of them. My mother's controlling herself better of late. Or at least she controls her tongue. She still
makes it obvious that she disapproves of everything I do. With
a shake of her shoulder, a tap-tap-tap of her finger, or a change
in the rhythm of her breathing. But that's alright, there's a kind
of secret pact between us now. She doesn't accept me, but she
tolerates me. I'm looking for a job. And I haven't met anyone
yet to relieve me of my body's magical membrane.

* * *

I've met a lot of artists at Lambo's. Pretty much all of them,
except maybe U, Ü, V, Y, and Z. Whenever I've brought up
poetry or politics with them, or tried to initiate a true friendship, as human beings are meant to do, or to earnestly engage
in discussion of a topic I know a thing or two about, they've
responded with teasing or mockery; they've evaded the words,

the topic at hand, and instead turned either saucy or outright aggressive. When I've asked them for help in finding a job, they've avoided me. I've taken no interest in any of them, other than that having to do with art, or human nature in general, and, frankly, the fact that they are men has been of zero interest to me. After some two years of experience, the conclusion I have arrived at about them is this: they wish to appear bigger than they are. And what about other aspects of their behavior? A. B., B. C., and D. F. go around saying I've hit on them but that they haven't reciprocated. Haydar told me all about the conversations they've had among themselves, when it's been just them, just the men. One of them even said that I was straight up ready for him. Ready. For what? Goddammit! And it seems one of them took me to his pied-à-terre the other day, too. Not R. R.'s own; apparently we went to M. E.'s. I caught hold of M. E. today. I'd never even met him before. I only know he writes stories. I was as cool as could be. I sat down next to him at the bar. I ordered a glass of wine from Lambo. "Dear sir," I said, "I hear you gave R. R. the key to your pied-à-terre and that he took me there, you've been telling this story right and left." I said this politely, in a low voice, into his ear. "Yes," he answered, graciously, "I have been saying that: R. R. asked me for the key to my pied-à-terre, said he was going to take you there." "You're lying," I said. "I know R. R. well, he's an honest poet, he wouldn't have lied to you like that." At precisely that moment R. R. walked in. He seemed pleased to see me and extended his hand. "One minute," I said, still very polite, before extending my own hand. "It seems you've taken me to

this gentleman's place, is that so?" R. R.'s face immediately fell
into disarray. "What on earth, why would I take you there?"
he stammered. "I don't know why, but it appears we went!"
I answered. Lambo snickered as he listened but kept his gaze
averted. "*I* took you there?" R. R. said, looking at M. E. as if to
say, "What have you gotten me into?" "Yes, you!" I insisted.
"An utter falsity, miss, I hardly even know you, and, well, the
impertinence of it all, miss! . ." "Sir, but you do know me, and
I know you, we've encountered each other and spoken here
many times—in fact, you even gave me signed copies of your
books, hoping to gain a new reader, and I even told you I didn't
think much of your poems, right over there, so was it after that
when you took me to the pied-à-terre?" "Yes, I mean no, those
things you described happened, but that's all!" he said. "So
I'm the liar then, huh? But that's what you told me," M. E. said,
naive as could be. "I was talking about somebody else," R. R.
said. "Fine then," M. E. said. Actually, M. E.'s a fairly honest fellow, he's not like R. R. I turned my back to them both, and they
soon got up and left.

—Isn't it shameful, Monsieur Lambo, do they imagine
   that I come here looking for men?
—Well, they're men, you know. That's what men are like.
—Are they trying to tell me, these cretins, that I should
   cling to my mother's skirts and not venture into public places, can they not see me as a friend, or as a sister?
—Hardly possible that, my girl, they're men, after all, and
   you're not their sister! . .

* * *

On the way home I struggled to arrive at a conclusion regarding what had happened. In front of Saray Bookshop, an enormous fellow suddenly began to follow me, kept repeating like a broken record, "A hundred liras, a hundred liras." He'd walk up ahead of me and stop and wait, then slip in behind me again. He was wearing a cap, had muddy rain boots on his feet and stubble on his chin, looked like a cross between a bandit and a thief. I didn't get angry. What was the difference between his view of women and that of our very own R. R., supposedly one of Turkey's greatest minds? Nothing. No difference at all, if you ask me. Compared with this guy, the others are far guiltier, of course. He sidled up to me at one point and showed me the corner of a bill in his pocket: *100 LIRAS*. I laughed. He grinned. *Perhaps I should bestow the gift of my little membrane upon this fellow?* I thought. I saw he'd drawn up really close now, and we began walking. But I couldn't stomach the thought. Just as we approached the policeman at Taksim Square, I said, "Come on now, why don't you tell this policeman what your problem is," and with that he spun around and took off. If only Halit were here. Halit's not like these guys. He's an actual human being, if only he were here today . . .

* * *

After classes today I went to a newspaper office. I'd heard they were looking to hire a jounalist. I went straight to the editor in chief. A young man. I explained to him why I was there and asked if they were hiring, and he seemed interested. He went in and out of the room and asked a few people some questions. One or two heads popped in through the doorway, looked at me, then disappeared. Finally he told me the position had been filled, but that if anything else turned up, he'd let me know. He asked me for my address. Said he was going to send me a letter. When I tried to excuse myself he insisted I stay, ordered us coffee, and told me he'd heard my name before. Curious, I asked how. "I'm very good friends with R. R," he said, smirking. "I see," I said, and left.

* * *

I ran into *Him* today. We nearly came nose to nose. I stopped, turned around and stood next to him, and then started walking in the same direction and talking. He's quite different from the others. He's not even on speaking terms with most of them. I told him I'd stopped writing poetry, "You were right, my poems aren't any good," I said, and told him I was looking for a job. "I'm afraid I don't know anyone," he said. "Actually, I'm looking for a job myself." What an odd man, such a sourpuss, always avoiding other people. I can hardly believe that he came to Çardaş once to read my poems and didn't even make me pay the bill, not even half of it . . . Leaving him, I continued on my way home and saw Haydar coming from the opposite direction. We went into Baylan's for a cup of tea. I told him what had just happened. "Don't pay any attention to him," he said, "he's not like you think." "What do you mean, like I think?" "He doesn't like women." "Well, so much the better—no way I'll let him get away now, at least that means I've found someone who won't be obsessed with my woman-hood." He laughed. "Well, more power to you," he said. I told him most of the poets I knew were either crazy or pretended to be. I said some of them picked it up in France, while others were just plain idiots. "You're right, they're all a little crazy," he said. "So," I asked, "is it these psychos who are to be the creators of Turkish literature?" "Certainly," he said, "them, and people like you." "You've never even read my writing, it's rotten stuff," I said. "So's the stuff they write," he said, and we laughed. I got up to go, and he moved to another table. A. I. was sitting at it. "Go on, tell him that you, too, took this girl to your pied-à-terre!" I said. He got so upset. I was sorry I'd said it. "You and I are friends. If you should ever doubt me, then we should never speak again," he said. I apologized. I told him it was just an ugly joke I'd made, still smarting from what they'd done to me. He held out his hand. "You and I are good friends, I wouldn't trade your friendship for that of any man," he said. I thanked him. We parted. What a beautiful thing he'd said to me. I felt blissfulish.

* * *

A letter arrived from Halit. I didn't get the one before it, it must have gotten lost at Lambo's. I doubt Lambo had any-thing to do with its disappearance, but it probably ended up in the hands of one of his regulars. Anyway, it's not like it contains any secrets. Halit's letters do always end on a passionate note, though: my love, my longing, my darling, my soul, my baby. Heaven knows what meanings others will read into those words. I'm going to write back to him right away.

* * *

Meral's father died of a brain hemorrhage. She missed classes for three days. She's a bit pale. We walked around together in the garden and talked, she says her mother is taking it very hard. "I'm quite upset myself," she said. Seems to me that she isn't really, but she's embarassed to say so. I know how much she used to long for her father to die, back when we were in high school. So in less than two years she went from that to loving him, the same father? I asked her about Bedri. "Oh, you know him, he couldn't care less." I asked about Ayten. Turns out she and Bedri split up. Ayten wasn't coming to classes anymore, either. Meral made me swear not to tell: apparently Ayten works in a brothel now. I was so saddened to hear this. I nearly burst into tears. This time, Meral was the one who consoled me. "She was already that way before Bedri," she said. I was stunned. How could it be? A pity, she was a good girl, really.

* * *

I picked up Halit's latest letter from Lambo's! . . We're finally running away. "Suppose I go somewhere far from our country, my friend, would you come with me? There is some danger involved, the danger of being caught, but it's slight. We'll make it, you'll see. We'll make it, and we'll be happy." Happiness together—does he mean as man and wife? Or in the friendship he mentioned above? "There's someone else coming with us, you must trust that person as you do me," he says. I became delirious with joy. Yes, of course, of course, I'll go. Who or what is there here to hold me back, to keep me here? I wrote back to him at once. I'm ready whenever you are. I don't have any money, but I'll get some from my mother, one last time. Or rather, I'll steal it. She can count it against future expenses she would have had to pay for me. There are a few hundred liras in the money box in the top drawer of the chest, I know. Worst-case scenario, I can pay it back once I'm over there and have a job. I wonder where we're going? He says he'll tell me later. I'm insanely happy. I have to make sure my mother doesn't catch on. She picks up when something is afoot, just by looking at you. If she catches on, I'll be done for. Ha ha ha, this will be a good lesson for you, madam protector of membranes, a very good lesson indeed.

* * *

Today, Mother and I went to Pendik to Meral's to offer our condolences. Mother never passes up an opportunity to weep, and when we got there they had a little festival of tears. Bedri was at home. He and Meral and I sat together in the L-shaped living room of their new house. Bedri's so tall now. He's a good-looking

fellow, something I hadn't really paid attention to all these years
. . . When I look at him, though, two things come to mind, and I
can't help but laugh. One is how he kissed me once, his mouth
still full of the cherry shortbread my mother had made, and the
other is the way he looked at me after Ayten had gone to the toilet. His eyes no longer have that old insolence. "Are you still boxing?" I asked. "I can't, not as often I used to, classes are really
tough this year." "And what about poetry? I haven't seen your
name in any of the journals lately." "Oh, I've given up writing
poetry, it's such a feminine pursuit . . ." I laughed. "And you, are
you writing poetry?" he asked. "No," I said, "I've left poetry to the
men." He laughed! "What are you reading these days?" he asked.
I listed all the books I was reading. "On whose advice, Halit's or
Halûk's?" he asked mockingly. I was terrified my mother might
hear and signaled for him to keep it down. "She can't hear us,"
he said in a hushed voice, and I responded, "I got recommenda-
tions from the both of them." I was angry with Meral, though,
seems she goes and blurts everything to her brother. I know he
wouldn't stoop so low as to tell my mother, but why on earth
does Meral have to go and tell him all my business... On the
way back home, my mother told me Aunt Nazife would have
to work as a seamstress now, that her husband hadn't left them
enough money to live on. "God forbid, whatever would we do if
that happened to us?" she lamented, about something that had
not even actually happened. "That Bedri, he's become quite the
young man, hopefully, once he becomes a doctor, he'll give his
mother a good life. A son is different. May God protect him," she
bleated on and on as usual.

* * *

There were flying ants all over the ground this morning. Spring has arrived once again. The weather's mild, I only need a cardigan now when I go to classes. I ran into Kevser in the hallway today. She gave me a smile. It was her way of extending an olive branch. I pretended not to see her. No, I'm not angry at her anymore, I'm not angry, but I can't be friends with that girl again. İncilay and I ended up sitting next to each other in class. She draws so beautifully, she drew a sketch of me in her notebook and then showed it to me. It was a very good likeness, and underneath she had written in English, "Who is the slayer, who is the victim." I was taken aback. I looked at her face. She was looking toward the lectern, pretending to listen. I have no idea what kind of girl this İncilay is. What could she have meant? I was curious. After a while, she began drawing in her notebook again. This time I craned my neck to look. It was a sketch of the lecturer, Sabri Esat, and on top she had written, "My Love." We giggled. Clearly this girl is a hoot. And here I thought maybe she knew something about me. She's sweet, though. I suppose girls like that are happy, and make those around them happy, too. Right?

* * *

There were flying ants all over the ground again this morning. There were so many, I had to watch my step to avoid crushing them. By the time I reached the corner I'd given up, and began stepping on them randomly. I looked straight ahead, to the sky, so I wouldn't see them being crushed. I suppose they've been given wings so they can fly, yet they still grovel on the ground, underfoot. They creep, with some difficulty, into holes in the ground, protecting their wings the whole time. How strange. Are they flying ants or creeping birds?

* * *

I dropped in at Lambo's. There was a letter from Halit. I opened it immediately and found another envelope inside. On it was written "top secret." I put it in my handbag and ran home. My mother was vomiting. She must be pregnant, she's having cravings, too. She says she never has these strange cravings when it's a boy, so must be another chit on the way. Anyway, I don't care, whichever one is fine with me. I asked her if there was anything I could do for her. "Stop breathing down my neck!" she screamed. I caught the lady in an act that was proof of her sin, you see, and now she was ashamed. My gosh, how on earth did this woman of such pristine virtue ever manage to give birth to me? Apparently it was the mere gaze of my father that knocked her up! I went to my room and opened the envelope; very soon, very soon now he's going to let me know the day and the hour. One day next week. "Whatever you do, be sure to stay at home next week, my dear," he says, "I'll send either a telegram or someone who will say he's looking for 'Quiet Lady Cul-de-Sac,' a short, dark young man in his twenties with a moustache. If your mother answers the door, he'll leave and return half an hour later, and this time you must be sure and answer the door yourself. He'll hand you a piece of paper, my soul, you'll find everything on it: the date, the plan for departure, a map of the roads to follow, what to take with you, where we'll meet." He signed it, "With love, Your slave." Slave! Never in the world!

* * *

Went to school early this morning to catch Meral before class. I often miss the first class, I read late into the night and only get there in time for the second. I tried to convince Meral to leave and skip class with me, but she wouldn't do it. Meanwhile the Crone walked in. So I had no choice but to stay as well. "No more classes today, we'll take the day off, extraordinary things are happening," I told her. "Spring has gone to your head," she said. İncilay sat beside Mehmet in the row behind us. I often see them together, they must be dating. I looked at İncilay, and she was looking back at me, laughing up her sleeve. I laughed back. She opened her notebook at once, began to draw, then lifted it up to show me: lots of spring blossoms on branches, and an enormous eye lurking among them, and underneath in English, "Not that I like the Crone less, but I love spring more!" That girl is a real devil. As soon as the lecture was over, I dragged Meral outside. "We're going," I said. "Are you out of your mind?" she said. "Yes, I am, now come on, hurry." She gave me the weirdest look. "I can't say any more right now," I said. We took a ferry at the bridge. We got off at Küçüksu and

73

rented a rowboat for an hour. It was a gorgeous day. Scalding hot, though, the Bosporus. We rowed ourselves out beyond the post office, near the pier at Anadoluhisarı . . .

* * *

This is a spot my mother discovered. We come here once a week every summer. We take a ferry from Beşiktaş and get off at Anadoluhisarı; walk past the park to the right of the landing, and those little side streets with their huge cobblestones by the foot of the citadel, and you arrive at a vacant lot with a view of the water. There's usually a few children already there swimming in the shallows. My mother wraps me up in a large towel, like a cylinder, and I undress and put on my swimsuit. It's one my mother has knit for me—the oddest garment, all sorts of colors—and it extends all the way up my neck and well down my thighs. I run to the sea like that, like some strange sea animal of my mother's creation. She sits on a blanket she's spread on the pebbles, without removing her beige overcoat, and she opens her black umbrella to shield her from the sun. "Don't go too far. The currents are strong again today, come this way. That's enough now. As soon as I hold the towel up, you start running. One, two, three, run." Then we return home.

Two little boys were rowing a red boat not far from us. That's where I told Meral. She was dying of curiosity. "I'll be gone next week, for good," I told her. She was shocked. Ha ha! I first made her swear on the head of her mother not to tell anyone, because she loves her mother and she believes in such oaths. She's not to tell Bedri, either. "If I told him, he'd stop you, he thinks of no one but you," she said. "You come, too," I told her. "Let's go off together, there's one more person coming along, so the four of us can pair off." "I suppose you're going to have to sleep with Halit," she said. "I don't think he'd force me to do it, but I'm prepared to do it if I have to," I said. "Well, it's got to happen eventually, with someone or other." "And you?" I asked. "Three months ago, I'd have tagged along," she said, "before my father died, but now there's no way I can abandon my mother like that."

A murmuring sea bathing beneath the sun, smooth as can be. We tossed the anchor overboard and lay down face-up on the deck. As the waves gently rocked us, we spoke as if in slumber. "No one's even kissed me yet, did you know that?" Meral said. "Necat?" "No, never. Once at the cinema, he wanted to kiss me, but I was scared, I wouldn't let him." "I've been kissed," I said. "By who?" "Your brother, Bedri?" "Did you two make love and not tell me?" "Goodness, no. Once, when we were children, he attacked me, and something kind of sort of happened then." She laughed loudly:

—You know, one time, I woke up in the middle of the night and thought, *Anybody, anybody at all.* I mean, ANYBODY *at all*, do you understand?
—How about the grocer boy? Or crazy İhsan from the old neighborhood?
—Now, they'd have been real pieces . . .
—You've lost your mind!

—Have you never felt that way, have you never been mad
   with desire?

—No, I can't say I have. What I have wanted, very much,
   is for someone to love me, but I mean really, truly love
   me, to be with someone really special . . .

—I'm not a virgin!

—You're spinning tales again!

—You don't believe me?

—You're going to make up some strange story again, I can
   tell!

—If you don't believe me come here and I'll show you.

—Are you crazy? I don't want to see! Don't even try, I
   simply won't look!

We both sat up at the same time.

—I'm not a virgin!

—Well, who was it then? Tell me. Those dreadful naval
   cadets, when we were in high school?

—No.

—Who then?

—Bedri!

I lay down on my back again and closed my eyes, then
opened them wide and looked at the sun until it blinded me.

—You don't believe me?

—I believe you.

—There was no one at home . . .

—Don't tell me.

—Let me tell you, I have to tell someone. I came out of
   the bathroom, I had a bathrobe on, and my back was

sore. I went straight to my bed and lay down, with the
bathrobe on. I was moaning. My brother came in. He
asked me what was wrong and I told him. He said, "Let
me give you a massage." I'm disgusting, aren't I?

—Alright, I get it, you're telling the truth, it doesn't matter, don't worry about it.

—You don't think I'm disgusting?

—No, not at all . . . I was a bit shocked at first, but even
that's passed already. It's normal, I mean it's human, I
mean it's completely plausible . . .

—We couldn't look each other in the face for days,
couldn't talk at all. Then it was just forgotten. We
became brother and sister like before, as if it never happened . . .

—So you didn't do it again?

—No.

My eyes opened. The sun beamed down on the oppo-
site shore, drenching the citadel's walls in white. The boys had
rowed their boat up close to ours. They were shouting, "Show
us, sister, come on, show us." We both stood up and turned to
look at them. I couldn't help laughing. One of the boys was sitting there in his underwear, the other in a jacket. When they
saw us looking at them, they shouted again, "Please show us,
sister!" "Show you what?" I asked. "Your you-know-what, sister, please." "The little bastards," muttered Meral, her eyes well-
ing up with tears. I didn't know what to do. The boys had rowed
up close. "Come closer." I lifted my skirt, pulled my panties
aside, and showed them. The boys whooped in astonishment.

"Aren't you ashamed of yourself?" Meral shouted at me. "No, I'm not," I said. Then I yelled at the boys, "Now shove off!" I pulled up the anchor and grabbed the oars. I hadn't been ashamed. I thought I'd helped alleviate Meral's shame. I didn't know what to think . . .

* * *

Meral wasn't at school today. I went to Lambo's. Poet A was sitting with N. When I walked in they gave me dirty looks with their bloodshot eyes. I didn't bother to greet them, went straight to a corner and sat down, grabbed the glass of wine Lambo handed me, and took a drink. Poet A was staring at me, our eyes met. "Who do you think you are?" he said. I didn't reply. It was obvious they'd both had a few too many. Lambo sensed something was about to happen and retreated behind the counter. He looked like a little boy come to church for Sunday service. A shouted again, "I said, Who the hell do you think you are?" "I'm nobody, but so are you, and here I thought you were somebody!" I said. A jumped up off his stool and stomped toward me. N caught hold of him, but he kept raging: "What impudence! Just listen to her! Go on, get out of here, what are you doing here, anyway, seeing as we're nobodies, huh?" "And who are *you* to tell me where I can and can't go?" I said. "I'll tell you, alright, now we don't want you here, so get out!" "I'm not going anywhere, who do you think you are, trying to kick me out, you think I'm going to live my life the way you want me to? You think you're going to dictate my life?

Who gave you the right!" "You bitch, get the hell out of here!
Don't make a man sin now, you slut!" "Your sister's the slut,
you bastard. A pathetic drunk, that's what you are." I stood up.
"These doors were opened for me by Atatürk, do you hear me,
you closed-minded bigot? Atatürk opened these doors for me!
Who do you think you are trying to force Turkish women back
into the dark caves of the past, huh?" At this he froze stiff, he
had no comeback. "Shame on you, shame! And to think I once
liked your poems," I said. And it's true, he's written some really
fine poems, the bastard. "But I was wrong," I added, "a man
like you can't possibly write good poetry. You're charlatans, the
lot of you, you speak of freedom and equality, but underneath
all that talk, you're just a bunch of old-fashioned bigots." All
this while Lambo was pleading with me, "Don't, please, sweetheart, the police'll show up and shut this place down, please be
quiet . . ." The police did not come, but the door opened, and
in walked Haydar. "What's going on?" he asked. But I wasn't
about to get Haydar involved in this, taking my side. "Nothing,"
I told him. He squeezed his fists, he's a big guy, Haydar; one
blow from him would have sent both of them sprawling onto
the floor. It's not a bad thing to be physically strong, it was the
first time I'd ever had this thought. A's attitude changed as soon
as he heard me say I used to like his poems . . . "Fill it up,"
he said, handing Lambo his glass. Haydar leaned over him.
"You got a problem, buddy?" he roared. One of his hands was
clenched into a fist. I grabbed it. "Never mind him, let's go, I
was just leaving anyway," I said, "the only problem they have
is with themselves, the pathetic creatures." Haydar released his

hand from mine. He stood up straight while A cowered, mumbling, "God forbid, God forbid." I opened the door. "I'll settle my bill tomorrow," I told Lambo. I pulled Haydar out with me. "Atatürk," I said as we left, "opened brothels so you men would leave us in peace, but he forgot to put the money in your pockets so you could afford to go to them." The door closed behind us. Haydar let out a hearty laugh. He looked at me and then quickly pulled his fingers away from mine. "I thank you," I said. "Heaven only knows what they might have done if you hadn't turned up, they were both stinking drunk." "Come, let's go to Baylan's and have something to drink, it'll calm you down," he said. We walked to Baylan's. I told him—I now realized that he was my best friend–that I was about to run away with someone. I made him promise not to tell anyone. "Have you thought it over carefully? It's dangerous, have you thought of every angle, every risk?" he asked. "Yes," I replied. "Are you in love with him?" he asked. I hesitated. "I don't know for certain about that, but I feel good when I'm with him. And I trust him. Actually, I know it may seem like I'm experienced in such matters, but the truth is, I'm not, not at all . . ." He reached out and stroked the hair on the top of my head, then pulled his hand away. "So this means I won't get to see you anymore." He paused. "You're such a child," he said. "You are a mischievous child." He paused again. "If you need anything, let me know, write to me, call me, wherever you are, and I'll come." He stood up. "Let me see you home this time," he said. We walked together to the corner of my street. From there I ran to the door, rang the bell, and then turned to look back at the corner;

from under his big felt hat, behind those dark glasses, he was looking at me. I shuddered! My mother opened the door. She and Aunt Havva were in the living room; Aunt Havva was reading Mother's fortune in her coffee grounds. I came up to my room. Now I feel like laughing and crying at once. But no, I'm not going to cry, I'm not going to let them get to me, not going to let them make me cry, I will stand my ground, and I will go back there . . . Those monsters' efforts to belittle me, to besmirch me, will be in vain, I'll show them. Thank you, Halit, thank you, Meral, thank you, Haydar. Without you, I wouldn't have been able to stand my ground today.

* * *

I went to school, ran into Halûk. He gave me a half-hearted nod from a distance then shuffled off. The bastard! And to think that only a few months ago I got slapped because of him. So inconsiderate—no, not inconsiderate, ungrateful! That mule, pig, mouse, toad, centipede, piece of shit!

* * *

Back to school today. My very last day. Tomorrow is Saturday, the day after that is Sunday, and then Monday. That's when I'll start waiting. Meral and I walked all over campus. We skipped all our classes. The cafeteria, the garden, the library, the stairs, the corridors, the banisters, we visited them all one by one. As a final stop, we decided to pay a visit to Lambo's. I asked Meral what her plans for the future were, what was she going to do? "Isn't it obvious by now: I'll finish school then start teaching, what other path is there for me?" she said. I asked her why she was so hopeless, and so resentful. "Don't act like you don't know," she replied. "You really are making such a big deal out of this," I said, "how *alla Turca* you've become recently! You're no different from my mother! If you, too, thought your honor was located between your legs, then it's a good thing I'm getting out of this country." "No, it's not like that, but you can't possibly understand: I didn't want to do what I did," she said. She was right. "Forget about it," I said. There was no one at Lambo's. "Come on, let's go to Degustasyon one last time!" I was so filled with joy, yet Meral was so sad, so miserable, I couldn't bring myself to leave her like that. At Degustasyon, the poets R, İ, K, L, and O were lined up around one of the tables, dining and drinking. "Goddammit, I'm in no mood to put up with them right now," Meral said. On catching sight of us, K leapt to his feet. "Ohhh, here come our anarchist girls!" he declared, forcing us to join them at the table. "Don't let them get to you—we'll have our own fun with these rusty old bogeymen!" I whispered to Meral. I'd heard about that old geezer K from Haydar, who'd relayed his words to me: "You have a go at them first, we'll get our turn eventually, I can wait." K raised the first glass to us, a lewd smile on his face. T lost no time in trying to ingratiate himself with Meral: What was she writing? Whatever it was, he'd see that it got published in *Varlık*—as it happens he and others at the table were about to put out a new journal, we girls absolutely must join the editorial staff, because Turkey desperately needed anarchists these days. "What makes you think we're anarchists?" Meral asked, obviously annoyed. "It's in your eyes!" L chuckled, and then they all burst out in laughter. Meral looked at L. "I'm not surprised. It's clear from the nonsense you write that your grasp of anarchism is limited to what you read in peoples' eyes," she said. This time they laughed even louder, mocking L. This rankled L, who shot back, "Of course, it's not only your eyes that give you away as anarchists!" expecting a round of applause. But the others weren't in favor of stooping quite so low quite so quickly, they had intended to reveal the extent of their nastiness only gradually and prolong the entertainment. I felt like spitting on the table and taking off, but that would've meant swallowing this insult. Meral's face was fiery red, angrily she turned to L, and I held my eyes closed for a moment, opening them again at the sound of Meral's voice. "In that case," she said, "in that case, you must be aware that among the most notorious anarchists out there is your very own wife?" L jumped to his feet, and there was a buzz of whispering around the table. This time I burst into laughter, and then everybody else started chuckling. They all knew that L's wife was R's mistress. L grasped the bottle in front of him. R grabbed his hand. "Let's go, you see what they're like!" Meral said. I pulled her down by the hand and made her sit. "We'll leave in a minute," I said. N proposed a toast to us, I raised my glass and took a drink. Meral didn't touch hers; she just sat beside me trembling, her forehead and cheeks red as a beet. "Gentlemen," I said, "is there anyone among you who would like to sleep with me?" Dead silence. They all started looking at at each other. Then they tried to force a laugh but couldn't. "I'm not joking," I said, "I owe you all, I owe you all so much. I have benefited from your friendship, I am all the richer for it. Two years ago I had no idea that there was a world like this one, where I am sitting now, not half an hour from my home, right under my nose. If anyone had told me, I never would have believed people like you even existed. Today I know all of you, each and every one. I've seen with my very own eyes the anguish that Turkish intellectuals suffer! I've learned how they view women. And now I wish to bestow upon you, of my own accord, something you would not be able to wrest from me otherwise, even if you labored at it for forty years. Choose one from among you. The poorest, most pathetic of you all! And I shall give him this as alms! For I have no need of it myself." "That's enough, stop it," Meral said, yanking at my arm. R got up and left. N turned to the others. "What on earth is this girl saying?" he asked. The others just stared, frozen. "My dear child, you've got us all wrong," the old geezer K protested. "We've no such design on you girls." "Oh yes, sir, you have," I said, "in fact, I've heard that you yourself have been waiting your turn." This time it was İ who burst out in laughter, while K uttered, "Good God!" then fell silent, and the others began talking among themselves as though we weren't even there, helping themselves with abandon to pickles and pastries. "Come on," I said to Meral. They pretended to be so engrossed in their conversation that they didn't notice us leaving.

* * *

"Why on earth would you do that sort of thing, have you lost your mind?" Meral said. "I don't know," I told her, "I don't know, but I felt love for them when I first met them." "You're very odd," she said, "sometimes I don't understand you at all, what you want to do, what you're trying to achieve." We fell silent. Then, "Did you see L?" she asked timidly. "He looked at me as though he knew about me!" "Oh come on, don't be silly, how could he possibly know," I said. "They just don't want to accept us. They don't want to see Turkish women in their midst, all their bravado about following Atatürk's revolution, it's nothing but pretense. Our being equal, coming around for the sole purpose of discussing art, of making friends with artists, is an insult to their manhood, they can't handle it, that's why they go wagging their you-know-whats whenever they find themselves in a bind. They're still Ottomans, these guys, Ottomans I tell you! Even worse than Ottomans . . ." Meral and I parted in Taksim. "I'll definitely write to you one day from wherever I end up," I told her. There were tears in her eyes. I arrived home. I sat down in the green armchair, and at one point I started thinking about Meral. It was a horrible thing that had happened to her, and she's such a delicate girl, she'll suffer from it till her dying day. My mother was in and out of the room, getting supper ready, pulling at the sofa's cotton cover every time she passed by. Protecting me from men, wasn't that her main worry? Concealing me from the enemy. Yet in the end to make a gift of me, as a wife, to one of them.

All the care she lavished to raise an angel, just so some monster might tear it to pieces. She's dressed up again today. For a moment I considered throwing my arms around her, telling her everything. What happened to us? What happened to my mother, the woman who rocked me in her arms when I was small, holding me tightly to her breast? I used to wake up each night and listen for the sound of her breathing, worried what would happen if she died. What happened to all of these people, to Halûk, to *Him*, to K and to A, B, C, and D . . ., to Bedri, to Meral? . . It's as if all of us have suddenly incurred the wrath of some vicious giant . . . "You're building castles in Spain, young lady, you're lost in your thoughts again, at this rate one day you'll get lost for good, now come and help set the table, Tayyar Bey and his wife are coming over for supper . . ." "Alright, just let me get changed first." I went into my room and cried. I'm going to be as patient as can be with my mother these last few days, so she'll cry even more once I'm gone . . .

* * *

Everything's ruined, in shambles. Nothing holds any meaning for me anymore. I'm in total darkness. Nose to nose with death. I've eaten nothing for two days. After a series of fainting spells, my mother has now started breaking into fits of weeping. She prayed to her Allah all night long one night, that she could die so that her honor might be salvaged. If only I'd been able to run away, if only I'd succeeded, then everything would be exactly the opposite of what it is now. I'd be happy. We'd be laughing . . . Whenever I thought of running away, hand in hand with Halit, sometimes fear would begin to overtake me and I'd almost change my mind. Yet now there's nothing I wouldn't do to be his. I have no idea what's going to happen next. I'm here in my room. I've tried twice to kill myself. I took the blade out of the razor I use to shave my legs. It had become dull. I ran it gently across the veins in my wrist. But I couldn't do it. I thought of jumping out the window. I opened it. I saw the Maiden's Tower, the Bosporus. The car ferry was leaving the Kabataş landing, and there were rooftops and houses and people and the voices of children. I can't even look down from a height, it makes me dizzy. Under the window is a tiny patch of land, a garbage dump really, we're on the second floor, it's not high enough to fall to one's death anyway. What difference will it make if I die? They'll simply say a girl of nineteen has committed suicide. Then they'll forget all about it. No, I am afraid of dying. Very afraid. I want to live. I want to live and take my revenge. Take my revenge, but on whom? My mother? I don't know. Is she to blame? No. Am I? No. I'm not, I'm not, I'm not. Right, but what's going to happen now? . . I don't know . . .

* * *

The doorbell rang, and I was first to make a start for the door. It was the third day of the week. My mother was in the kitchen. She walked right past me, looked me straight in the face, and said, "I'll get it." She opened the hallway door and went down the stairs. I listened from the top, heard a young man's voice say,

87

"Is this street Quiet Lady Cul-de-Sac, sister?" I nearly fainted. I ran back into my room. My mother came up the stairs. "Who was it?" I asked, "No one, wrong address," she said. I went back inside my room. I was trembling from head to foot. I looked at my watch. He'd be back in half an hour. I crossed to the guest room, where you can see the street from the window. There was no one on the street, so he must have been gone already. I started praying that my mother would leave the house or go to bed. I went to the kitchen. She was washing spinach. "Let me do that, and you go sit down," I said. The kitchen was the room nearest the front door. She turned to look at me. "What miracle have we here?" she said, then added, "What's the matter with you? You're deathly pale." "Why, nothing," I said, "I'm just tired of studying." "Well, you go on and study some more now, get those exams over with so you'll be free, and so will we." Just then the doorbell rang again. *The stupid fool couldn't even wait the full half hour,* I thought to myself. This time I got there first, I ran down the stairs and opened the door. It was him, Halit himself. "Does Nedret Hanım live here?" he asked as he pushed an envelope into my hands, a fat, smelly envelope. "No, she doesn't," I answered. He was smiling. "My darling," he whispered. I stuck the envelope under the waistband of my skirt and pulled my jersey down over it. "Read it tomorrow," he said, motioning toward the envelope. Then he caught my hand and kissed it. I quickly retrieved it, then I motioned for him to keep quiet and shut the door. I headed upstairs.

She was planted at the top of the stairs. I made for my room as though nothing had happened. After all, there was no way she could have seen us, the street door isn't visible from the top of the stairs. "Give it to me," she snapped, plunging her hand under my waistband. I tried to wrestle her hand back. "It's mine, Mother, stop it," I said. She slapped me in the face and grabbed the envelope, I clutched tightly onto one end of it, and a small corner tore off—that's what I was left with, and I pushed it down my front, she did the same with the bigger piece in her hand, and then bits of lilac blossom began falling to the ground between us. The sight filled her with fury, and she attacked me viciously. She pounded me with all her might, screaming like mad, "Lilac, huh! Lilac, huh! Lilac, lilac!" She finally stopped when she became too exhausted to continue, sank to the floor, and began to cry, "We're ruined, done for! We haven't an ounce of honor left, everyone will know, we are disgraced in the eyes of everyone . . ." she said, sobbing like a child. I ran off and locked myself in my room. I took out my razor, ran the dull blade lightly over my wrists, but I couldn't do it, I just couldn't . . .

—

I looked in the mirror. I'm like an animal. Exactly like an animal, a predator! A while later I recalled the torn scrap of paper and took it out: a triangular piece of a folded sheet, a large blank space, and just six words at the ends of two lines . . . *MY COUNTRY, I, BLUE MOUNTAINS, SOUTH* . . . From the blue mountains of my country I go south—is that it? From the blue mountains in the south of my country I—or this? Inside the envelope was another piece of torn paper, this one without any writing on it and thicker than the other, but with the same heady smell. It's not lilac, but a combination of lilac with some other smell. This second sheet was probably a map, our escape route. I threw myself onto my bed and began crying, though now my crying was more like a lion bellowing. I could hear her screaming from the next room: "Run away, huh! Run away! She was going to run away, the scarlet harlot, and with a Kurd no less! She has a lover, Allah take her soul, she has a lover! My daughter has a lover! What's more, he's a Kurd, a Kurd! . ." I heard someone knocking at the street door, the voice of the downstairs tenant, my mother snapping, "We're fine!" as she slammed the door in their face . . . I held the scraps of paper against my nose; that smell, that smell: *I've gathered this scent for you from the blue mountains of my country, with my own hands . . .* It's now the end of the second day. At midnight I unlocked my bedroom door and stepped out, my mother was asleep, my father wasn't home, who knows what he would have done if he'd been here, she's locked the street door and taken the key, I knew she would, but then where, to whom can I go anyway? . . I went into the kitchen, gorged on bread and water, then headed back to my room and passed out again. Nothing matters to me anymore, nothing . . .

* * *

A little while ago the doorbell rang. Meral's voice: "She hasn't been attending classes lately, so I got worried. Is she ill, Auntie?" I rushed out and came face-to-face with my mother, she looked at me with blank eyes, then ran sobbing to her room, I heard her lock the door. "Oh dear, what on earth has happened to you?" Meral said, wrapping her arms around me. I told her everything; she began to cry. "So you're stuck here, too, you couldn't get out, either," she said, continuing to sob, though whether the tears were for me or for herself, I'm not sure. "Stop it," I told her. "I cried, yet I didn't feel any pain, I was beaten, but I don't even know how I got these lumps and bruises. All I want is to escape, to find Halit." "Halit? What do you mean? Isn't he gone already?" "I don't know, Meral. There's no one left to rescue me but you, and I do not want to live in this house anymore . . ." "Wait, slow down, we have to think," she said, and pulled a handkerchief and a pack of Yenice cigarettes from her handbag, wiped her eyes, lit a cigarette for herself, and then gave me one, too . . . I showed her the scraps of paper, the bits of lilac, she sniffed them. "Ugh," she said, "they smell of oil and thyme." She laughed. "The blue mountains of my country sure smell nasty!" We laughed through our tears . . . Then suddenly, "I've got it!" she shouted. "I've got it, I've got it! Eureka, eureka!" She began jumping up and down. "Quiet, my mother could be listening at the door," I said. She perched on the edge of the bed. "You're going to get married," she said, "not for real, but you will, and then, in a few months, whenever you want, you can get a divorce, he'll marry you just to rescue you, you won't even have to sleep with him if you don't want to . . ." "Have you lost your mind?" I asked. "What man would agree to such a thing?" "Bedri," she said . . . "Bedri?" "What more could we ask for? He's mad about you, and as for your mother, she would be thrilled, and *I* would be your sister-in-law!" And at that she howled with laughter. "But will he agree to that sort of marriage?" "Of course he will, he'll be champing at the bit, we'll live in the same house for a while, then you can go off to Halit, or get yourself a job—at any rate, you'll be free of this house . . ." She left without saying goodbye.

* * *

Mother and I just got back from a shopping trip. We've been shopping for days now, I'm exhausted, and my feet are swollen from going to this store and that. Of course, they're not about to make do with some ordinary trousseau for me. Yesterday she ordered a rosewood bedroom suite. And today we bought this bridal dress. Mother and I can't decide if I should wear a veil, or flowers in my hair, or order a white hat from Margarit the milliner. My fiancé is really a very nice guy, truth be told, I've begun to warm up to him. My mother's very fond of her soon-to-be son-in-law, too, she's constantly singing his praises. My father was taken aback by the sudden engagement, but Mother soon got him used to the idea. "It's a good thing, a very good thing," she said, "that's how it is with girls, best to marry them off early." She didn't tell my father about what happened, she's kept it a secret. And there's been no mention between us of what happened, either, not since the day Aunt Nazife came to ask for my hand . . .

The other evening my mother gave in to Bedri's insistence and allowed me to go out to dinner with him and Meral. It was the first time in a month and a half that I'd left the house without her. I was drunk with happiness. We went to Lambo's. Monsieur Lambo was surprised to hear of my engagement. I asked after Halit. "No idea," he answered, eyeing Bedri. "You can tell us, Monsieur Lambo, we're among friends," I said. "I honestly don't know, sweetheart, he came here the once, been a good two months now, then I heard he was caught, sent back to his village . . . Maybe it's true, maybe not . . ." "In that case, write him a letter and be done with it!" Bedri said. "And his reply, how's he supposed to reply? . ." "He can write to you at my address, I'll see that you get the letter," he said. On the way home, Meral asked me, "Did you see that young man sitting alone in the corner? Guess who he is? Well, your Halûk, he's really done well for himself! He has his own studio in Beyoğlu now, a big one, and he's taken on that young man as his apprentice." Then she took one of her brother's arms, and I took the other arm of my fiancé, and in the darkness we proceeded toward our sacred institution of marriage.

THE FATHER

when you are dead they take your clothes
your friends and enemies are told
you are washed clean and laid upon
the funeral stone, all straight and cold

morning

I

Man has known fish since well before Christ, and then knowing fish, he also learned about trading, about boats. Well before Christ. How long was it, in 1707, since he had died? That year the Frenchman Denis Papin first conceived the steam engine. After James Watt's steam engine, Fulton built the first steamship in 1801. It was a side-wheeler, the wheels would pop right off in a heavy gale. Later the steam engine came into widespread use, on land and sea; the English began using ships to cross the Atlantic. The *Queen Elizabeth* weighs 83,675 gross tons. Throughout the Industrial Revolution, ship machinery kept veering from one course to the next, one course to the next, first alternating engines in 1840, then turbines, internal combustion (1894), and diesel since 1904. I won't be around for what comes next, because I am about to die, that's why.

—

The bright light of dawn wakes me. I no longer draw the curtains before going to sleep. As the sun rises I can see the acacia branches, then I watch the leaves move, as many of them as the window can hold. Nuriye's forgotten to unplug the icebox again . . . The appointed hour of death. I'm thinking of that, and also of Watt, and also of Fulton, and also of that ignoramus Sermet Vergin. My belly's full of water, swollen like a fat earthenware jar, that brothel-keeper says it's gas . . . These butchers, they're mighty quick to give a man up . . . It's the system, says Nermin. Nermin's my daughter. Nuriye chose the doctor, he's the military attaché's family doctor, that's why . . . Nuriye is my wife. Thank God our neighbor's son came to kiss hands at Bayram, he's just become a doctor; fork-legged Naci, he used to steal plums from our garden, he understood at a glance what was wrong with me. Naci was sweet on Nermin, before she married. "You've got water in the belly, uncle!" he said. I passed blood this morning, then stood, shaking, in the lavatory, and then I broke out in a sweat, the sweat of death, "You're dying, you're dying," I said, "Azrael's at your bedside— now just how will you die?" Nuriye took my arm and dragged me back to bed, I saw a glob of my bloody stool, she didn't flush.

She quietly digs her elbow into every visitor and shows them my bloody stool. Now she's got Nermin and my son-in-law in the loo, too. She's looked after me a long time, kept watch sleepless at my bedside for nights on end. If I die, she'll be free at last, she can sleep soundly then and breathe a looong sigh of relief! . .

For months I've lain awake all night long: the window, the iron burglar bars, the acacia, the sky. I watch the sky clouding over, the sky clearing up again, in the mornings it's just like it is aboard a ship, pinkish blue.

The pain's gone, it's gone now, cut clean away, as though with a knife . . . "Did my father see this?" asked Nermin in the loo. "No, he didn't." They think I can't hear them, but I can, I can hear every kind of noise a machine makes. These ears have made maps out of sounds, they were cozy with machines for fifty-five years: a tiny spring trembles, a bolt comes loose, a crank needs tightening, a ship—a ship, if only I had a ship, bow, mizzenmast, foresail, lower fore topsail, spanker, open the steam control valve, smell the condenser, check the steam gauge, keep an eye on the evaporator . . .

"I think he should go to the hospital at once." The son-in-law speaking. How can one die in this flyspeck of a house? Where would they wash the corpse, where would they put the funeral bench? My son-in-law's an X-ray specialist. They won't let me, they won't let me die in my own home. They came in feigning ignorance, my daughter sat at the foot of the bed, "Hello, Daddy, how do you feel?" she said. She always begins with a hello. Back in the good old days, whenever I came back from a voyage, she and I would throw a few back together, "Well, hello, Daddy, welcome home from the seas," she'd say, the son-in-law's standing there in the doorway, he's always there, always bored, a son-in-law who's like a great big broomstick, I can't lie, can't say I've taken to the guy, where in the world did Nermin find him, still, thank God for this one—imagine if we'd been stuck with that other one, the gypsy playboy? "How are you, Father?" he said. "As you see, my son." "You're just fine, just fine." "If I'm just fine, then let's have a glass of wine, why don't we?" They laugh. Go ahead, laugh, laugh away—you're not the one's about to die, how nice, then they're off to the telephone, to call the American Hospital . . .

Our seas over there are icy, summer and winter. Their waves strike the shore, rising more than thirty feet. It was on account of the Great War that the family migrated to Stamboul, they live in a mansion in Fatih. I'm here with Mother Romrom. I got through prep school, I know the Koran by heart, I have a sad, moving voice, when I went to Stamboul my older brother the captain sent me to the Gülşeni School of Music. Abdülkadir Hodja was my teacher, when I chanted the sacred verses the women would hide their faces in their handker-chiefs and weep, could be the tone of *hüseyni, acemaşiran* . . . Our house in the old country was on a hilltop. I say house, but what a house it was, more like a castle, with crenellations, and a tower! I slip into the Black Sea that climbs up the hill, the water takes me in and pushes me to the bottom, it froths and it slithers me up against the fish; since the Treaty of

London, the Black Sea fish are considered demilitarized; the gurnard, gray mullet, sole, turbot, plaice. What's the water up to again, it whirls the fish around and around, tosses me up against the mansion with a thump, I rise from the sea, not so much as a scratch on me—now at the mention of the sea, something is settling right in, settling right in here, and I rise and climb the hill again. Mother Romrom keeps pleading, "Don't do it again, I beg of you!" My father's first wife, barren, she sits on her haunches at the foot of the zorafina tree,* her eyes always wet with tears—my father'd just died after leaving the navy. Mother Romrom has hung his uniform on the castle's impenetrable wall, wrapped a handwoven towel around my father's shoulders, and his gold-braided sleeve swings empty against the wall. "Gimme those, Mother Rom, let me try them on, let me be a gen'ral!" But she won't let me touch them. It's hard times here now, drives people to strike out in search of more. I move to Stamboul for good, to be with my captain brother, the enemy's killed my other two brothers, he wants me with him. He's the head of the family now. My real mother, my brother, and I are going to live in that mansion in Fatih. "This is where I was born, this is where I'll die, you must bury me here in the garden, beside your father, under the wild cherry," says Mother Romrom. She refuses to come with us.

No one's answered their phone calls . . . It's Sunday . . . The

---

* Wild cherry tree.

doctor's not at home, either. The doorbell rang, Zehra Hanım's voice, our next-door neighbor—real windbag, that one—first Nuriye took her to the lavatory, they were whispering among themselves, *pssst pssst pssst pssst,* now they've come into my room . . . Ah, my wife's been crying! . . "Whatever's the matter, Hasan Efendi? . ." I can always tell when my wife's been crying . . . Her eyelashes, they disappear, and the look she gives—it's the look of a mackerel, my wife of forty-five years . . . She cried and cried, saying if my first son were alive, he'd be in his forties now.

She shed many tears when her brother died, saying "He was all I had," and then again when I talked of divorce, saying "I'll go to the grave before I'll be cast out to strangers," it was in Beşiktaş—not that I truly meant to divorce her, I just wanted to get her guard down—and again when our firstborn died, I thought she had gone completely mad: she clung to the corpse, kept repeating the refrain over and over, "My fair-haired boy, my fair-haired lion, Allah, make this earth a desert unto me, Allah, let me never know the love of a child," and then she'd be throwing herself against the walls the way they did in those romance novels she liked to read . . . She said "fair-haired" to stress that he took after her side of the family, 'cause my father-in-law was fair, they say; the Fair Aga they called him, this daughter of mine has taken after my side, the boy after hers, ever since that day it's a grieving woman that I hold in my arms . . . Ah yes, and that other time, when she thought me drowned out near Kefken, when we rammed into the shore, some newspaper had it that the whole crew had drowned, "Have you no pity on your orphan, Hasan?"

she sobbed that time . . . This, on top of everything else I've been through . . . That time, six of us, we rescued ourselves, squeezed onto a rock, there was Yakup from Mamul, Captain Kâzım of Istanbul, former cavalry officer, dead now. . . What with the storm on the one hand—the night, it was black as pitch—and hunger on the other, we felt ourselves beginning to freeze, from the toes up: I said to Yakup, "How about a *horon*, let's dance the dawn in," and he began making the sounds with his mouth, alone at first, then we all joined in jumping and leaping in dance as we sang:

> *Riv riv riv and riv riv riv and riv riv riv*
> *and riv riv riv*
> *The handle of my kemençe's of plum wood made,*
> *of plum wood made,*
> *I cannot bear to leave behind that pretty maid,*
> *that pretty maid,*
> *The rifle on my shoulder is meant the enemy to kill,*
> *Is this the moment to be stuck upon this lonely hill?*
> *Riv riv riv and riv riv riv . . .*

I got the six of us so worked up that we stomped on our piece of rock the whole night long, and toward morning, when a motorboat came and picked us up, Captain Kâzım was still hopping: swish whoosh swish whoosh! . . Whenever he saw me after that, he'd ask, "How about a *horon* to usher in the dawn, huh, chief engineer?"

She held Nermin to her bosom, "Have you no pity even for

your own orphan, Hasaaan? Are you buried at the bottom of the sea, no earth to cover you, Hasaaan? Have you been devoured by fish, Hasaaan?" Yet when we are alone, the two of us face-to-face, such airs, such cheek, you'd think she was the daughter not of a down-at-the-heels Albanian aga but King Zog himself. Never once have I known her to throw her arms around my neck and let out a fond "Oh, my darling husband," she's like an unruffled sea, standing straight and tall by the shore, like an ancient tree trunk, "Only the common folk do things like that!.." "You'll be fine, Hasan Efendi, just fine, Şüheda Hanım, she was just as bad, but she got over it." I shut my eyes real tight, "He probably wants to sleep, let's go to the other room."

When my sister-in-law first saw my brother the captain, his tall figure, his fair hair, his blue eyes, and his prodigious nose, she told him, "*You* will be the one to make me a woman, *you*, no matter what!" He bedded the Tatar beauty and married her. She fetched her grand piano, music books, and a bundle of clothes and moved straight into the mansion with us. In our house, the butter came from Trabzon, we had salted sprats, oranges, sacks of hazelnuts . . . I no longer take lessons from Abdülkadir Hodja. In the mansion I have my oud, my songs, my real mother . . .

> *There is no sorrow so great as that of separation*
> *Come join us and we'll have a wondrous celebration*

The neighbors all think I have a splendid singing voice, on

my neck I feel the breath of women sighing from behind their screens as I pass, when I ask for Nuriye's hand she comes running to me, she's only around sixteen at the time. She hasn't been there yet a month when we're struck by fire; the smoke is the blue of the Black Sea. We're able to salvage the *kemençe*, the oud, and the ceremonial sword my father wore when he appeared before the King of England. After the fire we're digging about in the ashes, when from the ashes the piano emerges all in one piece, my Tatar sister-in-law wipes her eyes, says "Bought with the honest-earned money of my late father!", over the ashes she hunches, and bangs out a tune, that's when my mother dies. She lies in Eyüpsultan now. When did all this happen, forty, fifty years ago? If I were to die right now would Nuriye hold back her tears because "Only common people weep"?

If I turned to look, raising my head from my deathbed, and heard them say, from just past my brittle shoulders, *Get up, start all over again*:

Buy a square-rigged *taka* with the money from the sale of the land. You, your brother the captain, and your uncle Memiş, a four-ton boat.

Load her up with gasoline in Romania, sell the gas in Giresun, get hazelnuts from there. Bring them to Istanbul.

Your uncle Memiş seizes the money from the sale of the four

thousand kilos of hazelnuts, you and your brother the captain end up with the debt—he couldn't care less that you are the children of his sister.

Uncle Haci Mahmud Efendi, a lieutenant in our navy fleet and the battalion imam on the battleship *Turgut Reis*, receives his salary of forty-five liras and gives it to you out of pity.

Rent a house at Tabak Yunus, install Nuriye and the Tatar sister-in-law there.

Go buy a secondhand rowboat for 170 kuruş, row passengers between the butter market at Yağkapanı and the pier Yemiş İskelesi.

The money's not enough, send Nuriye to the old country to stay with Mother Romrom.

The Tatar sister-in-law dies of tuberculosis, leaving her piano behind.

Sleep in a dilapidated room above İsakzade Ahmet's wooden coffeehouse in the butter market, five kuruş a month, you provide the bedding.

Make six to ten kuruş a day. (A loaf of bread, 1,120 grams, costs one kuruş, a stale loaf only thirty para, make do with a stale loaf.)

At noon eat a plate of beans (twenty para), eat a plate of rice (twenty para), eat three hundred grams of bread (ten para), pay fifty para in total.

Another fifty para for the evening meal.

Have a coffee (ten para), a tea (ten para), a dessert or a lemonade, something cold (another ten para).

Three kuruş a day for food, live this way for two years. Clothes, the rent, and your clothes get real dirty.

Ready set GO, don't die, Come On, Go!

DON'T DIE.

READY SET GO!..

ONE TWO.

ONE TWO ...

Wait, that's not all: with his winning ways, and by getting you false papers with a two-lira bribe, your brother the captain gets you a job on the SS *Osmaniye* of the British-registered Egyptian Khedivial Lines. Begin your seaman's life as a stoker on the Istanbul-Alexandria run at three pounds sterling a month.

When the Kuvayi Milliye is formed at the end of the First World War, go and enlist together with your brother the captain.

Load the supplies given to you by the secret society in Istanbul onto your ship (the *Crimea*), transport and deliver to the Kuvayi Milliye at the Samsun and Trabzon harbors.

One time, about ten miles short of landing at the Samsun harbor, be stopped by the Greek torpedo boat the *Eraks* and armed transport the *Naxos*.

Have two Greeks lash the *Crimea* to the stern of the *Naxos*. Have them lower our flag and hoist their own blue and white.

Have them land you and the passengers, children and all, onto İğne Island and ransack the *Crimea*.

Forty of you spend that night in a coffeehouse.

In the morning have an army bayonet escort of forty take the forty of you capable of bearing arms and march you to Kırklareli, which they call Kırkkilise. Have them march you that day and every day for sixteen hours, with forty cartridge belts as whips to strike you forty times to cries of "*Vre kayimeni turkospari, hathite palioturakaldes!*", spitting forty times, pissing forty times at your Turkishness, have them march you till the blood seeps from the oozing wounds on the soles of your feet, they keep you marching, marching, marching, marching, marching, marching . . .

ALL THIS FOR THE SAKE OF THE HOMELAND!

Have them put you in a POW camp in Piraeus for two years!

You save this country now, you idiot! Do your part now—save it!

GO!

READY SET GO!

ONE TWO THREE FOUR, ONE TWO THREE FOUR!..

With us, navigation and smuggling developed simultaneously. It was shipowners from the Black Sea who were responsible. A seafarer hailing from the Black Sea begins with a small sailboat or a *taka* but, after coming into possession of a steamship, turns almost exclusively to smuggling. They smuggle mostly opium and heroin. The fathers of these men, who are presently counted among the top tier of our country's wealthiest class, paved the way for their sons and grandsons to become what they are today, primarily by means of force majeure robbery: You claim the general average on your cargo. You make for a port, claiming your cargo got wet or was washed overboard. A truckload's worth of carpets (cargo) is removed from the ship. That's force majeure for you . . .

You see, our merchant fleet is developing in just this way, that goes especially for Hamit Mordon's diesel tanker, he belonged to a dervish order, that guy, was one of Abdülkadir Geylani's disciples, a real fine fellow. During the war he made us transport guns to Chiang Kai-shek, secretly, and the second year he bought a second tanker, he starts talking and there's no doubting his humanity, he brings tears to your eyes with all that dervish wisdom, I'll never forget, he lent me a thousand

liras when I bought this house, a proper human being . . .
Fine, and? Well, we did as we were told in those days, of
course, heels smarting, tongues held, we had homes to support, we waxen galley slaves. Galley slaves, that's right, that's
what Nermin calls us. We kept quiet. If we hadn't, we would've
starved, but then one day I looked up and, what do you know,
there were so many ships, so so many—if I couldn't find work
on one, surely I'd find it on the next—and so I'd stick a cigarette between my lips and, cheery as could be, I'd walk up and,
"Well now, skipper!" I'd say, "Cough up my wages and then
give me the boot if you like, thanks to us we've got democ-
racy in this here country now, I can't tell you what to do!" Is
Nermin right, who knows? If only she wouldn't overdo it! My
shoes wear down, it's because of the system, she says, Mahsune
Hanım is caught with her lover, it's because of the system, she
says, a ship sinks in a storm, it's because of the system, she
says. "This socialistism of yours is a fine thing," I told her one
day, "Man can do no wrong, no matter what happens, it's all
because of the system!" I explained to her our religion, the
matter of God's will and individual free will, these people have
just found an easy way out—oh, how I laughed that day . . .
"Being silent is not demeaning, it does not mean surrender,
does not mean bowing down!" my brother the captain used to
say. "You may have to bow down and make an escape, but only
to gather strength for the charge and counterstrike," he'd say.
"Though, if you overdo that bit, well, then you'll really be up
the creek, don't say I didn't warn you!" I was around ten when
he started bringing me up, he's my father and my brother both.

I cannot forget, no I cannot! . . He said once, "Just how many sailors' lives you think would be saved if you made an MP of me, huh?" He said that, and they laughed. He could speak his mind to any man, no matter how harsh, and meet with nothing but a chuckle, because when he spoke, it was heartfelt. Now, I'm not sure about speaking heartfelt, but when I lose my temper, I sure do curse heartfelt. He never got angry, I never knew him to raise his voice, and for this reason everyone loved him, though what difference does it make whether they love you or not, here I lie in the throes of death, no matter whether I was ever heartfelt—who helped my brother when he died? . . Once he made me lose my temper, wouldn't stop asking, "Who killed Suphi?" As though he'd gone mad. Toward the end, he'd walk up to anyone and everyone and whisper in their ear, "Who killed Suphi?" As though he'd gone mad. I lost my temper and in a right heartfelt rage I told him, "To hell with your Suphi," and we quarreled, and he died still cross with me, my brother the captain.

Yes, they've found the easy way out. I had a good laugh that day. Right here, in this house of ours, is where I'm going to die. I've made up my mind, I'm not going to the hospital. We sat on the glassed-in balcony we'd added to the front of the house, father and daughter, and lit our cigarettes. That's right, I'm no bigot, I let my daughter smoke in my presence, like a European father, in those days she always wore a black skirt and a black blouse . . . It was a fine day, like this one, the acacia fluttering its fans in the breeze. Nuriye's passion flowers climbed the garden wall; the Atatürk flowers, poinsettias, glowed in their earthenware pots; sweet marjoram, fuschia, begonias, zinnias . . . The sun hung over the bare plot of land opposite, painting the tall grass coral pink, the smell in the air was like we have back on the Black Sea coast, a scent like salt purple, that when it touched Nermin's cheeks, or her hair, became a pink smell, that day when I looked at her, I understood why the neighbor's son Dr. Naci had been in love with her—her bright shining eyes, her soul-baring voice—looking at her like that, all the blows fate had delivered over the decades, the filthy waters of decades of struggle and suffering seemed to flow out of me, I was washed clean. I harbor no hatred, no resentment toward anyone. She looked me in the face and understood me. "Well, Daddy," she said, "you've made your house, and you're in it, you're looking out at the garden your beloved wife has filled with flowers, lighting up a cigarette, your daughter comes to visit you—it's almost like you aren't that same galley slave of fifty years ago, like you've forgotten all about the past . . ."

That girl just can't leave well enough alone, she's always making waves. I kept quiet, decided to let it slide, put it down to her childishness, but she insisted: "If every citizen could lay claim to seventy square meters of space like this, to three rooms and a little garden full of flowers, educate their children and give them a start in life, and end up with a nice little pension of a few kuruş every month, wouldn't that be nice?" she said . . . I kept quiet . . . "But most of them can't even fill their stomachs," she continued. Look at her now, just look at her, she won't let herself be loved, she refuses to be happy, as though happiness were something repulsive! . . "There must be some whiskey in the cupboard, from your last voyage," she said, "shall I pour us each a glass?" I spoke to her like my brother the captain, didn't raise my voice, spoke without anger, heartfelt. "I'm not supposed to drink, I've got water in the belly," I said. "What kind of water?" she asked, turning pale. "What kind do you think? Must be seawater, of course," I laughed. Her face trembled, her eyes became rage, became the back of a monkfish, "Those rotten scumbags!" she cried, leaping to her feet. "Didn't that Dr. Sermet Vergin say it was only gas? Rotten doctor, rotten system!" she began. She clenched her fists and shook them up and down in the air as she shouted like some third-rate Bolshevik. "You just go on voting for them, why don't you." (It was nearing election time.) "It's all their doing, you've forgotten what you had to put up with on their filthy ships—the rotting food they forced down your throat, the wormy chickpeas, the fruit full of maggots, food they wouldn't deign to give to their dogs . . ." She continued her rampage. "Hard astern!" I cried. "And you tell me: have they gotten rid of cirrhosis in Russia already?" But she wasn't listening, "It'll pass, it'll pass, it must be stopped, it simply must, it must . . ." she said running to the telephone. She herself wasn't aware she was weeping: rows of tears trickled down her cheeks, I was startled—she loves me, my daughter loves me—then my eyes welled up, and I cried, too. She phoned her husband, between them they got hold of this new doctor, a true son of the people! It's him they're phoning again right now . . . He was born in Anatolia, he doesn't look down on people like us, he'll do everything in his power, this doctor . . . Sometimes I look, and what I see, the things they think of, the ways of dividing people, what happened to them to make them so distrustful; they are the children of the Republic, Atatürk and us, we left them a country with no enemies, they've known neither war nor famine, they haven't been prisoners of war, or beaten up by Greeks, no infidel flag has encroached on the green shadow of their ships. What doctor, what child of Atatürk, would refuse to look after me—the soles of whose feet are covered in the scars of deep wounds—would knowingly do me harm because we weren't of the same class? . . Their friends are just as bad, I've talked with some of them, they're going to take revenge for us all, they say! Something happened to the world, it seems, while I was out at sea, something happened to the world I left behind, something happened, but what?

The door . . . Nuriye goes to open it . . . It's Melek Hanım, the military attaché's wife, our other neighbor, the most genteel resident of the neighborhood, the one whose family doctor is Dr. Sermet Vergin. Nuriye thrusts even her into the lavatory, where my bloody stool is awaiting spectators. Now Nermin has joined them. "Cirrhosis? Maybe it caused the bleeding? What do you think?" She exhibits polite surprise. My wife: "Of course it's cirrhosis, of course! My dear Melek Hanım, cirrhosis, the disease of Atatürk!" Nermin: "The only inheritance that my father has come into!" "How dare you!" Her mother is shocked! Those two can't get along, they're always at each other's throats. Just what will you two do once I'm dead? My wife started up with the weeping again, blowing her nose like she does. Then they came into my room. "How are you, Hasan Bey? I hope you feel better soon!" "I'm fine, just fine, Melek Hanım, you keep an eye on Nuriye from now on, won't you, see to it she's not abandoned." They all looked at me in wonder. "Well, now, illness is just part of life, mind you, comes and goes, you'll be free of it in the end," the woman said, stupidly. My wife began sobbing at that point, so they led her out of the room. Nermin didn't go with her, though. When things get tough, that girl grows hard, her blood freezes, there's that saying, "a wet fox doesn't feel the rain"—that's exactly how she is. She sat down at the foot of my bed and began looking at me, slowly moving her gaze, beginning with my feet, past my legs, up my *kemençe*, my *kemençe* stem, my chin, lips, nose, eyes, eyebrows, forehead, hair, ears, she reached out and took my hand, which was hanging out from under the quilt, and felt my pulse. "Do you have any pain?" she asked. "No, I'm fine now." From where she sat, she fixed her eyes past her legs onto the carpet. I'd guided many a ship into the harbors of that carpet. I blurted to her just then: "So tell me, Madam Nermin, does Allah exist or not?" She slowly turned her head and looked at me as if she'd been waiting for that question, her eyes brimming with tears, she remained silent, we'd debated the topic a thousand times before, I waited. "Well, come on then," I urged, pretending to be angry. "How should I know, Father, and this isn't really the time, is it?" she said, her voice strangled. "What do you mean, it isn't the time, it's not like I'm dying!" I chirped, and she pulled herself together, became her old mulish self.

"You know what I think, Dad," she said, kicking up her hind legs, "there is no Allah, there are only the exploited and the exploiters." Would you look at this girl, knowing her father's on the brink of death, yet she can't even bring herself to admit the existence of Allah just to make the poor man happy before he dies, you'd think she wasn't my daughter but that of some Armenian verger, the little devil! If you can't bring yourself to say *Allah*, then call Him *God*, call Him *Dieu*, call Him anything you like, say it in mulish, but say it, just say it, your father's seen all the colors of the rainbow, he's a smattering of half a dozen alien tongues, now say something, for God's sake! . .

Yet she knows, yes, she knows the pain I suffer because of this, how I eat my heart out (*stick a pin in my skin*). It's my fault, that's right, my fault, I should have taught her how to have faith. They think faith is surrender, that it's submission. Resignation to God's will only makes things easier for others, so they say! They're unable to grasp the profundity of finally possessing the strength to turn your back on the false blessings of this world, they don't understand how to rise above, how to reach maturity, how to attain the perfect state.

They fail to realize that this quest for truth together with everyone else in the form of socialism is a lowly endeavor. Their aim isn't to surpass others, but to be equal to them, they say, they'll have time for philosophy after they've gotten their rights; while the rest of us were lost in soul-searching, they say, our leaders turned themselves into wealthy shipowners . . .

Ha, a lot of codswallop! How many times have I told her about Mevlana Celaleddin Rumi, how many times have I said to her, "Yours is not an elevating task, if you really do not wish to be like everyone else, then why do you limit yourself to the prevailing ideas of the age, everybody's a socialist nowadays, why not look for something beyond, aim for perfection, you'll get nowhere by insisting that you're going to make them pay," but no! . . She won't have any of it! What a shame! . . What a shame! My poor child! Whoever's responsible for making her like this, may he suffer for it, the ten fingers of my two hands will be at his throat on Judgment Day! If she could only have a little faith, if only I could've lit that divine spark in her soul, and she is so smart, so smart—the doctor measured her head top to bottom when she was born, said this child's going to real smart. But what use is being smart if it doesn't make her happy, if it leads her astray even? All that restlessness, that throbbing heart of hers, her lack of love, that lack of love will do her in one day; she'll collapse facedown on some shore—it cuts me right to the quick—from lovelessness, it's the lovelessness that will be her undoing most of all, for she has said to me, "I loathe any favors that this system claims to bestow," she said, "We won't forgive what's been done to you, and others like you, we'll make them pay, and if not us, then those who come after us will make them pay, they will make their children pay!" They're mere kids, they think it's easy! And besides, who asked you to do this, did anyone ask you to take revenge for them, did they, for someone to thirst after vengeance like that, they must have gone through real hardship, eh! But they're just full of hatred, full of it (*stick a pin in my skin*), and if someone is so full of hatred . . . a person can die of hatred, die of it! . . No, no, we must believe in Allah, He's a refuge, a support, a consolation . . . And it's not that He's in the heavens, necessarily . . . I've explained that to her as well, I told her He's inside of you, He's everywhere, in water, wind, and fire, I said:

> *Neither in Right am I, nor in water, wind, or fire,*
> *Neither in heaven nor earth, the mine below or the world*
> *above.*

I told her, "You're an Allah," I said, "every human is an Allah." "I only want to be a human, Dad," she mocked me . . . I haven't brought my child up as I'd have liked, I couldn't do it, struggling on the high seas to earn the family bread, I haven't looked after my darling as I should have, she was left to her mother, and all her mother taught her was how to knead, how to embroider, how to make lace . . . They're crazy, every one of them; Goddammit—mornings she sweeps the house from top to bottom, afternoons she shouts in the public squares, evenings they're all drinking rakı in the taverns . . . Well, if philosophy, if higher matters were reserved only for the wealthy, then how come we've thought so much, believed in so much, among all the wars, prisons, famines, how, how, how I ask you, how, huh? . .

Evliya Çelebi said of the Black Sea, "According to historians with knowledge of nautical astronomy, it is a deep

sea, eighty fathoms deep, and a black sea, the residue of
the dark waters of Noah's flood . . ." Fed with the waters
of rivers like the Kızılırmak, Yeşilırmak, Sakarya, Çoruh,
Dnieper, Dniester, Volga, and Danube, burying the oldest
civilizations on earth with its 2,200 meters, a vast plain,
according to Spindler, filled with 462,563 cubic kilome-
ters of water, bitter here, salty there, sweet in some places,
its color restless from yellow to green to deep blue to purplish black. A fault line parallel to the sea between Hopa
and the shore emerged in the undulations of the Alps. Its
soil is suitable for corn, oranges, red cabbage, wild cherry,
hazelnut, and, at the end in the east, tea and tea alone.
When Mehmet the Conqueror, one of those slayers of his
own kin, took Istanbul in 1453 and the Ottomans built a
powerful naval fleet, the Black Sea became a Turkish lake
and successfully stayed off-limits to foreign navies and
foreign commerce. Unbelievable.

The Russo-Turkish War, the War of '93 . . . After the War of
'93, the Black Sea, the Black Sea again. Batumi is left to Russia;
the *peçuta** recognized Russia after the signing of the Treaty
of Küçük Kaynarca and became liberated fish. According
to *Kamus ül-Alâm*, the entire population of the district was
138,423, of which 689 were Rûm. Is there Rûm blood in my
lineage? Nuriye says no more than four generations back we

---

* Bonito.

have Rûm blood, Greek I mean, "Despina's seed," that's what
she calls Nermin when she's angry, by Despina she means
Katherina, the daughter of John IV who married Hasan the
Tall, Hasan who fought against the spawn of the Ottoman
brother-slayers, so supposedly we are the guilty breed! . .

Ah, that must be Captain Tahsin, I can tell from the way he
rings the bell, presses down so hard you'd think he's trying to
wake a sleeping anchor watchman . . . "What's going on, chief
engineer!" he asked, sweeping into the room so fast my wife
didn't have a chance to push him into the lavatory. "Welcome,
Captain Tahsin, how are you, how's your heart?" "Managing,
for the time being, but, well, one more heart attack, and I'll be
off, too!" "How's that, is there a traveler due to depart before
you?" "No no no no . . . just a manner of speaking!" he stammered. The son-in-law walked in. "We are absolutely good
for nothing, nothing will become of us, nothing I tell you, a
useless nation, none of the calls are going through!" he said,
wiping his brow and standing by the door, taking the place of
the broomstick. "That's the way things are under this system,
why don't you try calling to report a malfunction?" Nermin
chimed in, to the rescue. "I'm in no rush, I'm better now," I told
the son-in-law, but he headed off to the room with the telephone again. Nermin flumped down in the middle of the bed,
started taking my pulse. My wife yanked at the captain's arm,
had to show him my stool, too . . . "What's the count?" I asked
Nermin. "Seventy," true or not, who knows? . . Do these people really love me, what's underneath all this concern, they're

impossible to understand, are they paying off a debt because I looked after them raised them as best I could, are they trying to prove they're for the working class, or is it none of these? Seventy's a good count, I feel very sleepy, perhaps it was all a mistake today, and I'll get well . . . Even after a forty-eight-hour watch I used to go the harbor, straight to the harbor, to Constanta . . . What a woman, who-ho-hoa! Her eyes, golden, and those cheeks—when she spoke you'd have thought shad were swimming into the sea: she'd open and close the water, make it flicker and pucker, and she was like that herself, like uncaught shad, all fins and scales and thorny spines . . . "He's asleep, Mother, be quiet," she says, if you ask me, they're all crazy, these young ones, need to be held down and given a right good beating, right good, see if they don't go yelling for Allah and the prophet then . . . Crazy, crazy . . . She took all those broken vases, bent metal trays, old braziers, pierced copper jugs (*stick a pin in my skin*), even the Tatar bride's piano as her dowry, but now she scoffs at them. "What business do we have with a piano," she laughs, they're all affectations to her, our sacrifices are just bourgeois affectations, *crazy*, that isn't quite the word for her, *spoiled brat*, no, that isn't right either, she's sitting on my rug, on all my harbors:

Mahangâvur,
Çürüksu,
Kobuleti,
Kranji,
Canton,

Lima,
Rio de la Plata,

her eyes are fixed on my ships,

    the *Altay,*
    the *Adalet,*
    the *Kırlangıç,*
    the *Hocazade,*
    the *Ümran,*
    the *Raman,*
    the *Hacıoğlu.*

She strokes my hand from time to time, she's watching over me, if I get well . . . I'll drag her . . . I don't even believe in it, but . . . I'll drag this girl to one of those hodjas, have him pray over her, breathe on her; I'll get my child back if I get well . . .

Back in the old country, tuberculosis, rain, and hookworms are abundant. There's no sun. The hookworms may be due to the use of fresh human shit as manure, according to our Dr. Korkut; could be, though, that those driven to Russia by hunger to work in the mines and tunnels brought them back. When hookworms became rife in the mansions of Istanbul, on the Islands, in Therapia, and Beykoz, they said: It's the people from over there who came to Istanbul looking for work that brought them, why don't they just stay put, it's not like we go to their towns, do we, each to his own house, each to his own village, and besides, what about their oil, copper, zinc, manganese, the Genoese exploited it back in 1355. And what about Vasilaki, Yani Yuvandi, Siraioti, mined four thousand tons of ore before the First World War, let them do some mining themselves, and stay out of Istanbul!

I said to my brother the captain, "Why did you bring me over here, they don't want us." "Is it their fathers' land?" he said. "This country belongs to us all." I kept my mouth shut. Go back, if you like, to your father's house, to the shade of the wild cherry tree, tuberculosis, tangerines, oranges, and, after the Republic, the nursery, the nurseries and the tea, yet the root of that oil is still rivety-riv-riveted to the bottom of the sea. Back where we're from, the cast-off land of four sultans, our homeland. Wrenched from the Genoese—back then noble princes traveled back and forth to Crimea conducting their trade in broadcloths, gala robes, dolmans, waistcoats, while we wore baggy trousers, wound turbans of cheap calico, turned to the sea for our trading, and there fished for *hamsi* (*hamsi*, our fish that appears with the *hamsin* wind that blows in the wake of darkest winter), we salted *hamsi*, sold *hamsi*, there where in the time of Sultan Murad nine thousand of us Black Sea sailors . . . In dories and caramoussals, in galleys and bare hulls, we drowned and drowned in service to our country. In the Black Sea, of which they say to the forlorn, "What's wrong, have your ships sunk in the Black Sea?" "He's delirious," she says of me. Who's delirious, as if I don't know all about her delirious raving, her whole life long: that fellow she thought she was going to run away with (*two ferries scurry what's their hurry communist pasha*), then that other playboy (*communist pasha bring my boots won't you please*), that mackerel shark with the featureless face (*the boots the boots they're in the trunk*), Dad, we're getting married, he's a socialist movie actor (*the trunk the trunk goes in the basket*), that beanpole barged in, made himself comfortable like some gussied-up broad at a wedding . . . Blathering idiot, midwife must've pissed a potion in his mouth . . . I'mma in love with your daughter's miiind . . . I'll rough up that mind of yours, alright; I listened and listened, nothing but horseshit, brought some wastrel to your father, you nincompoop, I saw red, got up, and went to see one of his movies, dressed like a woman he was, all giggly, letting the man of the house pinch his bottom, must keep calm like my brother the captain from the heart, must speak so my words, they pierce her soul delicate sad palpitating, I began with the voice I use when chanting the Koran . . . Most sensible speech of my life I held forth:

My child! The honeyed tongue hides a sting in its tail (*stick a pin in my skin*), choose him who makes you weep, not him who makes you laugh, keep both feet on the ground, they say, but you keep kicking, don't you? (*Belberiça belkutitça.*) In all of Istanbul, this giant city you know all too well, shitty history and all, this Istanbul (*I dispensed with the rod tatulitça*), this Byzantium, virgin widowed of a thousand husbands, for which I myself composed a song in the Persian style:

Gentle as only whores can be
City of rank iniquity
In every pore hypocrisy
No particle of purity

That's how it went, so in all of Istanbul *this* is the son-in-law you find for your father is it, this gypsy playboy, this prissy belly dancer, befit, does he, the dories of your noble ancestors, the swords of your grandfathers, the sable furs of your forefathers, this belly dancer?! Be worthy of the upbringing I have given you, do not disgrace me, let my labors not be in vain, cast no stones into the bread that sustains you, my child . . . Before I could finish, she was up and gone. She sent me a message through her mother, said, "I'm over eighteen, I can go with whomever I like." Sure, right. I burst into her room. "I'll show you eighteen, you driveling Damascus devil, you," and I smacked her twice across the face, I treat you like an English gentleman sailor, and you spout off like some vulgar Laz lass, "I will run away, you'll see," with that I ripped up everything she had, every last bit, her sweaters and skirts, her coat, when I couldn't tear her shoes apart I threw them out the window and into the garden, as far as I could, they landed firmly in the snow heels up, I ransacked the whole house, I swore up and down at Nuriye, then flung myself into my bedroom singing that song of mine:

In every pore hypocrisy
No particle of purity

She locked herself in her room, didn't come out for days, didn't speak to anyone, didn't eat or drink—"I'm heading out to sea"—didn't even wish me Godspeed. We went to Natal that time, and I wrote her a tender letter, sent her a postcard, on my return I took her in my arms and kissed her, held her tight, and from then on she called me *Daddy*, it was *Daddy* this and *Daddy* that . . . Still, thank heavens she finally settled on this puffed-up mooncalf, so at least I don't need to worry anymore . . . "Don't, please don't wake him up, sister, I'll come back when he's feeling a little better," Captain Tahsin leaves.

- —To the hospital at once, the doctor said we should move him as gently as possible, they're going to give him a blood transfusion.
- —Tell me the truth, son, is he in real danger? Don't keep the truth from me.
- —No, don't worry. Of course, he's lost a lot of blood, but he'll recover.

(Like hell he will.)

- —Oh no! The foundation of my home is collapsing, the fire of my hearth is extinguished, my one and only life companion is departing this world!
- —Please, Nuriye Hanım, what if he opens his eyes and sees you like this!
- —Let's get him out to the car, nice and steady.
- —Wait, wait, I'm going to change his pajamas, my darling husband.

—Mother, this is hardly the time to be bothering with pajamas.

—It's best not to move him around.

—They're in the chest drawer, bring me his blue pajamas.

—Mother, forget about the pajamas, I already told you!

—I'm not sending him off like this for everyone to see.

—Oh, for heaven's sake!

—You don't give the orders in this house.

—Okay then, fine, go on and change him.

—I certainly will, and with my own hands, if he doesn't wear them at a time like this, when will he.

If I could speak, if I could utter one word, just a drop—but my tongue won't budge, or I can't move at all, I'm not sure—I'd like my striped flannelette Sümerbank pajamas . . . I'm able to open my eyes, can these wretches really be throwing me out of my own house, can you imagine, never seeing my room again, that crack in the middle of the ceiling from the Adapazarı earthquake, the walls that Hüseyin Efendi painted white for me, and that hole there, that hole, no matter which room I'm in, whose head is that moving back and forth, that voice, that prayer, who are these quivering lips, in which I find myself slipping in and out of sleep (*stick a pin in my skin*): Hayriye Hanım's adopted daughter was caught with a policeman, she let him in through the balcony door, and he got her pregnant . . . Is this the room? .. This crack . . . This hole . . . Is this eye my son's eye? Do I have a son? My son, my blond son, did he die? This is my room, the icebox across the way, on top of the chest that box, tin, I've had with me on every ship since the *Justice*, it's my sewing box, a ship, if only there were a ship now, a small pair of scissors, two spools, I unravel the tangled threads whenever sleep escapes me, in my cabin . . .

—

LES SEULES CIGARETTES
TURQUES AUTHENTIQUES

on one side,

CONSTANTINOPLE
CIGARETTES RÉGIE DES TABACS

on the other,

DES TABACS DE L'EMPIRE OTTOMAN

inside the lid, all gilt lettering, and what gilding it is, not a single corner peeled even after all these years. Samsun tobacco back then, I used to roll cigarettes from that Samsun tobacco so green, Samsın, Amisus Byzantine Rome Rûm Greeks, in their lap it grew, leaf with a short fiber like a pin, several pins (*stick a pin in my skin*), one spool of black cotton, one of white, razor blade, buttons (*belberiça, belkutitça*), my work overalls, down in the bilge, they got torn, I got some new ones at Ras Tanura, was it my son or was it my blond horse Kızbeni with

the white fetlocks (*I dispensed with the rod tatulitça*), my ship
where is it,

My aga has the keys
What does my aga want
A bird with a golden head,
I crossed seven mountains
Found seven keys
Who knocks at my door
As loud as you please
It's Halil's little Musa
With stubby arms and knock knees
One swift kick and he was down
His nose buried deep in the ground . . .

hurt

II

Summer will arrive early this year. The sea will brim white, its incense rising into the sky, the blond locks of Pola Negri growing more golden with each whip of the wind. From what direction will the storm approach, waters raging, the *kozkavuran*, the *turnageçen*, the *hamsin*, the *kokolya*? They will arrive without me. An early summer this year, the blue of the sea will brim with white, I won't be there.

These blue pajamas, this icebox, with the son-in-law still planted in front of it. I brought them from America. On the *Bakır*, the *Bakır* was a "society steamer," before it ceased being a "society steamer" and joined the State Maritime Lines—we were the first Turkish ship in American waters after the war. Me in American waters, downtown at Macy's, year nineteen what was it. In 1935 on the *Üsküdar*, a storm broke out in Zonguldak harbor, a rumbling noise, the smokestacks went sideways, cracked and fell off, filling the harbor with broken smokestacks, the ships, the sea all covered in smokestacks—it was '36, February of '36 in Zonguldak, a big sea grabs hold of us and starts bashing us up against the pier, grabbing and bashing, grabbing and bashing, wounds the ship, the wound grows, the hold, the engine room, arms, legs, they all begin to bleed, the ship runs aground, smokestacks, smokestacks, smokestacks . . . We send divers down to patch up the wound with canvas and paunch mats, we caulk her on the inside, and the *Kalkavan* tows us to Istanbul, water enters through the wound, near Ereğli blood flows, the Black Sea turns red . . . (The Black Sea I saw like that once before, deep dark red, off Trabzon, at the spot where Suphi drowned . . .) The owner told us, "What wages? You worked, you got fed, you also wounded my ship, cut off her smokestack, and sold it, consider yourselves paid, now go on, shove off . . ." Nermin vows, "We won't let them get away with it!"

I got transferred, together with the *Bakır* from "society steamer," to the State Maritime Lines, the bonito swam down the Bosporus when the Treaty of Sèvres granted unconditional freedom of passage in war and peace, melting snow got into their gills, they ended up in Sirkeci . . . The *Bakır* was in Sirkeci, too, providing city ferries with coal like a coal bunker. A snowstorm pushed it toward the pier. We were about two meters from the landing, and the space in between, some ten meters long, was filled with sleepy bonito, so numb they came up to within half a meter of the surface . . . We men, we men were hungry . . . Hungry as could be . . . An iron rod, three meters long . . . I thought of hookworms, sharpened one end with a file, and bent it into a hook, made it exactly into the shape of a hookworm's hook, I'll never forget that feeling of joy, I went down to the pier and began to fish with my hook—one fish, then another, then another . . . sixty-four *peçuta,*[*] I slung fifteen of them into a sack and took them home, pickled and salted two kerosene tins full. My captain brother, he was captain of the city lines' Kadiköy ferry then, the widower of the Tatar with the piano, he was at home, on leave . . . In his handwoven nightshirt, made of *peşkir,* he was amazed: "Well done, Hasan, how did you get hold of so many fish? Well done to you, well done!" I distributed the rest among the crew, they were happy, so happy . . . From there we went and sailed off to America, that's life for you: massacre fish to fill your tummy, get light blue satin pajamas and an icebox from Macy's, and bring them back home . . . I always told my daughter . . . But I couldn't get through . . . I said you can't pluck people from their lives and divide them into left and right, make them feel disgust at their own experiences, you can't get the better of them by belittling what they've been through, so many parts of life, sound of the zurna, cigarettes, the whir of the icebox, what's that noise, the twang of Orhan Boran's violin at noon, kidney pain, drinking in Tuzla, weddings, prison camps . . . You

---

[*] Bonito.

can't do it, living by logic alone will drive a person crazy, you frighten people, you think there's no such thing as a Muslim who misses the ringing of church bells, you can't cut a human being in two . . . What is a human being? . . A human being. Georgian, Noah, Mingrelian, Laz, Arab . . . Am I Tabriz, visited by Marco Polo in 1294 and Ibn Battuta thirty years later? Is not every human being part Armenian, part Russian, part Tatar, part Greek? Allah bids us to forget our origins. The Armenians, according to Assyrian chronicles, were in Arbela, and if they as the most ancient of the great sovereigns, if they succumbed not to any yoke since the time of the Sumerians, I ask you, have I succumbed? No. No one can charge me with this . . . Allah wants us to forget our origins, to be left with nothing but our humanity, he makes us lose our origins, he melts us . . . I sent my wife to the old country and joined a band of guerrillas, maybe that's why Allah has visited His curse upon me; a people of Caucasian, Tatar, Pontian stock who don't know their own language, don't speak it—broken, they've forgotten the language that was theirs for centuries and kneel before Atatürk, the Gazi. Identities, should they be inscribed in stone? Carved in marble? Like that of Darius in the mountains at Ecbatana (Hamadan)? At least on the doorways of houses, as they are on tombstones? But houses don't last, they're wrecked, destroyed, homes dispersed, people driven in swarms from this place to that. Doubtful origins, dubious stock, Mother Romrom used to say, and I who have left a story at every harbor, and, after the Russo-Turkish War of '78, left Batumi to the Russians, because my father

was the best sailor in the Ottoman fleet, standing like an *eşkina**
in the very front row when the king of England arrives. The year
is nineteen hundred seventeen. Even before Mustafa Kemal
begins the national struggle, we're in the Abu and Fırtına val-
leys, and I set the first heroic example; pieces of my body and
shrapnel rain down from the sky, Laz mothers carry ammunition and arms to kill the Muscovian heathen, with a few old
Mausers and a hunting rifle I fight an entire army, under the
command of gendarme Lieutenant Kahraman Bey, also from
my hometown, a man of Rize . . . I am a handful of men from
Rize, I've died on the slopes of Taşlıdere protecting the homeland, the occupation commander stands before the blessed
corpses of my martyrs and gives a salute: "Bravo, that's how a
soldier should die, on his own!" After these martyrs became
martyrs, their pockets were searched, a few kuruş were found,
a fountain was erected at Taşlıdere, and onto those kuruş was
written:

> Draw a line, don't leave a sign
> Write two and three, one and two
> That the wise may see wherein the fault lies
> We are sacrifices to this land
> Come to this martyrs' fountain
> Say a fatiha, extend in offering a bowl
> To the revelry of the houris

---

* A kind of fish that lives in the Black Sea.

I was under occupation for months, and in March of nineteen hundred seventeen our magnificent army came and rescued me, meanwhile commander of the Eastern Front Vehip Pasha had set up his headquarters, on the Harşit River; we wrote these words on the fountain, we saw the captain off (retired General Muhittin Salur), and in Rize he set up an ad hoc democratic government with the people (they call me "the people") and provided its security, I'll never forget Sadık Uluşahin's forty-fifth-year radio speech (by then we had radios) . . .

That speech—I left my cabin, turned right, and walked straight ahead, paced back and forth a few times beneath the mizzen-mast, then stood beneath the flag staff, watched the propellers thrashing at the waters, saw a thousand and one shades of the water's green, went back to my cabin, and while writing in my log en route to Karlskrona, on the *Seferoğlu* steamer, at the three thousandth mile away from native waters, I listened to it on the radio, with misty eyes . . .

The triple tails, the triple tails gambol in the waters astern, frisky, quarrelsome, spry, the weather's clear, we're on course, it's fine like this, very fine, sea and sky, sky and sea . . . We were amazed by the sight of that enormous store. It was the *Bakır* that got us there,

"IVY CLIMBING TO THE SKY, FILLED WITH AMAZEMENT, AMAZEMENT, AM I," and the pilot fish trailing us all the way, those American women are all over the place at Macy's, they're the ones who do the shopping over there—Karoleen, Dawly, Joody—I said give me those blue pajamas, she held them out straight at my face, she trembled . . . It's cold, which of the cold months is it, "what's he saying?" they ask each other,

> Sixty, watch the beams,
> Seventy, stop up seams,
> Eighty, fill the pails,
> Ninety, rig the sails,
> One hundred,
> November's at an end,
> Summer's around the bend . . .

you wouldn't understand anyway, but why are you decking me out like a heathen corpse, am I to appear before the people's doctor as a prospective bride, get away from me, let go of my collar, I half opened my eyes and saw them, sniveling around me . . . My blue eyes . . .

Look here: a member of that race of men whom Şemseddin Sami described as blue-eyed, red-complected, fair-haired, hook-nosed, intelligent, and hardworking but given to idle talk is about to die . . . For no reason of his own making. My son-in-law's face has thickened, my wife, the granddaughter of Sinan Pasha, wallows in misery at not being married to a military attaché . . . Is that why she was cold toward me? I doubt it .

.. She's got me into the bottoms of my pajamas ... Sinan Pasha was obstinate, cruel, vengeful ... For months now, it's been boiled zucchini, boiled beef, and stewed fruit for me, rakı and turbot for the rest of you, but wasn't your doctor of the people going to make me well, huh, where are my sprats steamed in herbs, my Rize cheese, my grape jelly, I'm departing this world hungry, hungry, I tell you ... A child of the people, you say shamelessly ... And just whose children are the others, huh, whose are they, shamelessly she tells me straight to my face, "You're a worker, Father, you have to accept this, or you'll be a traitor to your class, Father! .." "Off with you, off, may you die alone, damn you—*you* may be a worker, but my grandfather was a chieftain, my father was an official, he wore naval epaulettes, his grandfather received one hundred thousand aspers when he retired ..." "What difference does all that make to you, the day your boss fires you, you go hungry ..." I shout at her with all my strength, heaven and earth resounding with my voice, "Hungry is what you are, you spawn of cruel Sinan, bullheaded you are, you're the one who's hungry—does nothing have value for the likes of you; your forefathers who fought against Hasan the Tall, who stood up to Mehmet the Conqueror—are the castles they built worthless, just what is deserving of respect in your books, to become rich like the others, to enjoy life like the others, isn't that what you all really want? Does communism mean lack of respect towards your elders, toward everything, is that it, huh? Who taught you this degeneracy while I was out feeding my soul to the oceans, huh?" Her mother comes running at the noise I make. "Hush, dear husband, quiet, I beg you, the neighbors will hear, we'll be disgraced!" "Ha! That's right! Be disgraced, disappoint the military attaché's wife, you've made this girl what she is, she has the nerve to stand before her father and tell him, 'You're a laborer.' Laborer. Well, that's what she is, a laborer—*she's* the laborer! . ." "Don't get riled up, now, don't get riled up, I'll tell her what needs to be said, she's still a child, she repeats what she's heard, whatever she picks up here and there, you don't think she's your equal, now, do you? . ." Her eyebrows leap up and down on her forehead, they always do that when she's upset. So I begin to pick my nose, seeing her forehead like that. I always pick my nose or clean out my ears when I'm upset—it drives her mad—just so she'll get good and mad, look at how she's raised her daughter! . . Why did I send that girl to school, so that she would talk back to her father, so that she could belittle him, and she's still belittling me, still doing it, they drop in to see me, don't eat this, don't eat that, well, goodbye, and they're off to the party headquarters, or somewhere, up to no good . . . I'll tell you what, if that socialism of yours leaves no time for your old fathers, well then I shit on that socialism . . . She does this to her father, who's bowed down to countless curs just to bring her up? . . My wife puts a clean, freshly ironed handkerchief on my knees, I shove my finger all the way up my aquiline nose . . . "Please don't do that, Hasan, I beg you, take your finger out of your nose!" Her eyebrows are now leaping up into her hairline . . . "Aw, and why should I take my finger out, last living descendant of Ferhat Aga?" I say to her, —another of my

wife's sorrows is that her line's about to be extinguished—
"must you all meddle with my nose as well? Or do you think
only the working class pick their noses, huh? I fart on your
advice, take that!" These words will drive her insane, I know,
she flies into a rage, "Merciful God, grant me the patience to
bear this man's wickedness!" she says, bolting from the room.
"Nermin, girl, come here at once, Nermin!" she yells, she'll
take it out on the girl, and she can be right vicious when she
hits her, "What have you been up to again, you vile hussy? . ."
The girl screams. "Why must the two of you make me suffer so, as if that mad buffalo weren't enough, now I have to
put up with you, you strumpet, beating on and on like some
infidel drum, class this and class that, if you don't think
we're good enough, then get out, go be the upper class yourself, Despina's seed, degenerate creature! . ." My girl! I cast
the handkerchief from my lap and leap to my feet; she has
the girl's hair wrapped around one hand, and with the other
she's slapping her in the face . . . "You Rumelian Gypsy, you
talk of infidel blood in my family, do you huh!! . ." I let her
have it with all my might, "Help, help!" she shrieks, escap-
ing to her bedroom, she locks the door behind her, Nermin's
sobbing her heart out, I can't free my hands, "Please, Dad,
listen to me, you have to go to the hospital, you must, you
have to get well?" Her head is bleeding, blood streams down
her face. . . "I caused this, I caused this, Mother! Mom, oh I
caused my mother to be beaten! . ." They're sobbing. "Pure
ignorance, I should have stopped this, Mom, Mommy . . ." I
free my hands. "Shut your traps stop sniveling now I'm not

going, I'm going to die here in this house, right beside you all, is that your eye bleeding, why's your hair all over your face, why're you crying like this, I've never seen you cry like this before, I could never bear to look at you anyway; it's better to die, but in my own home, in your arms, at your side, in this room, this harbor, these seas, lift me up, that's Poti over there on the rug, don't step on Poti, you have to plug that hole, throw the cat out, don't let her look at me, spring on me, what did I tell you yet what have you become, you pay no heed to anyone, 'Say what they will,' that's your refrain, 'Say what they will,' have you any idea what those sons of bitches in your circle said behind your back, what friends from back home have said about you? Alright, never mind, stop crying, 'Your daughter's become a commonist, gives it up to any man who comes her way,' how bitter for a father to hear these words, I told you, before death, and you said, 'I won't let those people wear me down, I'm not interested in that sort of thing, anyway, my reckoning is different.' Well, what about your reckoning now, has it been vindicated? Don't cry, don't cry, now, just tell me if it's been vindicated or not. If it has, tell me so I may die in peace, I've been waiting all this time, waiting and waiting . . . What's it to you, what I've suffered; so his son studies in Switzerland—fine, let him, he gambles away thousands of liras in one night—fine, let him, I say, she's stood there staring at me for years, she wants to know the truth—what truth?—she wants to know where the guilt lies, while I've tried to teach her beautiful things, the oud, the rhythms of that song my Tatar sister-in-law worked so hard to sing:

Once more has the beloved wounded me
Fate, you cannot provide a remedy . . ."

May the body of Medeni Aziz Bey lying in the Çürüklük
Cemetery rest in peace, we buried my captain brother in
Eyüpsultan next to my mother, we were sore with each other
at the time, when was it? When exactly did my brother pass,
still cross with me? . . All because of those Bolsheviks . . . I
don't care for the Bolsheviks, not because they killed Enver,
bullheaded Enver, no, I even donned the Enverian headgear,
our wise Black Sea wanted to swallow it, wanted to send it
back, didn't want to steal it from me, that he might not mount
that white horse, might not wield his Afghan sword, might not
attack the Bolsheviks, be riddled by the bullets of machine
guns, oh no, oh no no no no, he was going to go, he had to go,
because he'd had his fortune read: "O, you—you shall command armies, defeat all enemies, be crowned . . ."

Let not he who bears the crown of the sultanate be vain,
For many a sultan's felt hat has the autumn wind swept
away

. . . he wore the felt hat of the Janissary, the headgear of the
dervish, the turban, the fez, the kalpak with a crest, why don't
I like Bolsheviks well I was in Novorossiysk, the year again
the date, nineteen or twenty, when they were celebrating
Bolshevism on the First of May, our people were in Ankara
celebrating the First of May under the auspices of Atatürk, I'm

in Novorossiysk, we're on the *Sulh*, red girls come and toss us into blue troikas, sailing through the air on wings, singing a song, "Workers we are, great labor's darlings we are," into our very laps, they came all the way to Giresun in the First World War, vodka, caviar, the *kazaska*, the balalaika, that's when I was wounded, the shrapnel flying in the air, kopecks, silver, *manat,** but where does the blame lie? Is this girl mine? Why's she waiting here? She sits facing me, waiting for the truth, waiting for the blame . . . We're taking Mustafa Suphi to Sinop, on the *Bahricedit*, my brother offered him a cigarette—he's around forty, forty-five, smokes a French pipe, a strange guy, wears a tie, spectacles, skinny, keeps playing with his mustache. Many wear such mustaches nowadays, I knew *osvobozhdenie truda, chernoe more*, the Kemalist kalpak, *gromki*, and *vodki* before she was even born . . . Why is it that I am a traitor to my class now? These words, too, newfangled, degenerate! In the old days, treason was for those above, not for the likes of us . . . And now? Now everyone's a traitor, everyone's an informer, in his last days, my brother Ahmet could think of nothing else, he kept asking over and over, "Who killed Mustafa Suphi, who killed Suphi? . ."

---

* An old form of Russian currency.

Captain Ahmet

III

The sunshine sweeping across the wheelhouse was mirrored on the elbows, knees, and seat of his government-issue navy blue uniform as Captain Ahmet of the Kadıköy, a handsome man in his forties with red cheeks and blue eyes, a man who always had a story to tell and whose sallies provoked storms of laughter in his listeners, directed his ferry away from the landing. As she bumped her plump stern against the heavy piles, Captain Ahmet felt a strange grating inside himself; a thought along the lines of "Oh no, I've hurt my ship" swept over his heart; then he gave a vengeful look at the general who stood on the landing staring at him.

The general:

"I didn't want to have to tell you this, but that's how it is, Captain." He shouted these words toward the paddle box, hands cupped around his mouth . . . Then, although he was in civilian clothes, he lifted his hand

to his forehead and gave a military salute to the ship,
and the ship frothed its stern at the general: Kadıköy–
Kınalı–Burgaz–Heybeli–Büyükada. She had embarked
upon her Büyükada–Heybeli–Burgaz–Kınalı–Galata
Bridge run. "Sefer, hey, Sefer!" the captain shouted at his
quartermaster. "Yes, sir?" Sefer answered without budg-
ing, his eye fixed on the water he was about to cleave.
"Tell me the truth now damn it: you didn't hear about
it?" "No, not at all, sir, I swear." "This is bullshit, damn it,"
said Captain Ahmet, looking at the silvery path ahead of
the ferry. "Give me that wheel. Now go below deck and
ask every one of the crew who Suphi was, who killed
him." Sefer silently surrendered the wheel and went
down the ladder two steps at a time, straight to the ship's
steward. "Coffee with sugar," he said.

Who wants to see his wife, his daughter, with shovels in
their hands, loading coal onto ships in the harbor, who wants
his girls sailing away in a troika, on the First of May, sitting
on workers' laps, his girl who's become Tamara, Dunyashka,
Manushka, Netochka? Don't step on the carpet.
Begin at Batumi
Makhinjauri
Kobuleti
Shekvetili
Grigoleti
Poti
Ochamchire

144

Army of godless workingmen . . . Allah bids us forget our origin, our creation, yes, forget slanting eyes, prominent cheekbones, yellow skin, red skin, green skin, the tall and fair, the short and dark, and all be as one, He torments us in order to make us forget, only Allah can find a man guilty, only He can convict one of treachery, and now these, these good-for-nothing upstarts, have the nerve to stand before you . . . You can't do without religion, my uncle Hacı Mahmud Efendi, the imam on the *Turgut Reis*, in his day the armed forces had the strength of religion behind them . . . Every Turk isn't an Atatürk yet . . . We buried our friend Recep the Hobo, one of the immortals, on the banks of the Sakarya, with a *simit* in his pocket and his Browning in his belt—his pistol, a Nagant, we sold, I took a bullet at Sakarya when my horse with the white fetlocks and the yellow eyes threw me, her name was Kızbeni, "Beauty Spot."

Kutaisi

Gudauta

Pitsunda

Gagra

Leselidze

Khosta

Tuapse

Sochi

My uncle Ömer Efendi was falconer to the sultan, the historian Ahmet—yes, this is history—they say he'd pretend to drink but pour his drink onto the ground, they say 1914 is a date, Zigana's a mountain pass, America's a place . . .

Kabardinka

Sosnovka

Novorossiysk

Anapa

Halfway there are we yet, and to the Mim Mim Group[*] my captain brother Captain Ahmet. He turned sharply to the general: Why did you hang Ziya Hurşit? Why did you have Osman Aga shoot Ali Şükrü? Make an aga destroy a Turkish soldier, a man destroy a man, why? Who killed Suphi?

Shingilik

Plavshanka

Kerch

Mariupol

Feodosia

Rauf Orbay was prime minister, you put him ashore, whom did you take on board in his place?

Kozi

Utes

Sloska

May you drown in a lake of your tears, if you didn't do it, then who did, was it Latife Hanım, was it Latife?

Alushta

---

[*] The abbreviation of "Müsellah Müdafaa-i Milli," Also referred to as "MM" in Turkish but pronounced "Mim Mim." Literally meaning "Armed National Defense," it was an intelligence group that collaborated with other intelligence groups against enemy forces during the Turkish War of Independence and was dissolved after the war, on 5 October 1923. (*t.n.*)

Bahchekale

Sevastopol

Hurzuf

Odessa

—What did Suphi do to you that you killed him?

—It's you people who killed him, the man said.

—If he'd come fleeing from the east, you'd have thrown him to the Kurds.

—Well, well, well. How could I know, but now let me get into parliament and you can have your people shoot me, too!

—Who's to say it wasn't the Bolsheviks who killed Suphi, too!

They laughed.

—There aren't any captains in parliament, don't go slamming the door in my face.

—I got to get this ship moving, you piece of surplus cargo—look at the hems of these pants, look at this worn-out uniform, I'm the one taking care of my brother's wife and daughter, you kept him out of work for two years after the POW camp, now he does nothing but chase after women, doesn't look after his family at all, now get your ass off my ship!

The general didn't quite blush, but his face did turn a shade of pink, and he disembarked. As my brother slowly guided the ship from the wharf, he felt a strange grating inside himself. That evening he stopped me in my tracks:

—Tell me the truth: did you kill Suphi?

—Have you lost your mind! Wasn't I a prisoner of war then?

—Never mind the prison camp, it's your excuse for everything. Now out with it.

—Look here, come to your senses, so many men have died; Mother Romrom has died, my father has died, my mother, my son has died—what's Suphi to me! If anything killed him it was the collective conscience of the nation.

—A lie, a lie, this nation has no collective conscience to commit murder with, besides I need a single guilty person on whom to wreak my vengeance.

—I saved fifty-three souls on the *Havran*, now what is Suphi to you, much less to me!

—I knew him, I'm the one who brought him to Sinop on the *Bahricedit*, we drank rakı together, ate purple cabbage. He was the movement's favorite, the apple of their eye, someone, some one man alone, killed him! You killed him!

—Go to hell! You lunatic!

He grabbed the *kutavi** and brought it down on my head:

—Get out of my house, you traitor, I never want to set eyes on you again!

He looked after my wife and daughter right up to his death. One year, I'm on a voyage again, on the waterfront at

---

* A long-handled wooden cooking spoon used for stirring.

Constanta, the asphalt is warm underfoot, I've fallen for Pola Negri, what can I do, I love her, "Pola!" I cried:

> *You are a bottle sparkling on the river's shore*
> *A delectable meal I wish to eat forevermore.*

She's wearing a tulle nightgown, her body shines like gold, her golden eyes sparkle, she even speaks a little Turkish! And when she asks, "Me, pottle?" . . .

My brother the captain was docking his ship at Heybeliada. He felt faint, made for the deck, desperate to get some air into his lungs, caught his foot in his frayed trouser leg, and stumbled, he's said to have said to Mevlût, his ship steward of twenty years, "Look here, son, off with you, I'll do the sweeping here in this fine suit of mine, you go find out who killed Suphi." Sefer safely docked the ship at Heybeli, they looked for a doctor on the island, but there was none, one of the passengers said he was a medical student, that he could help, he felt my brother the captain's pulse and cried, "He's dead!"

Mustafa Suphi

IV

Xenophon Analus tells of a Greek soldier in the eighth century before Christ, was it? On foot from Babylon. Mud-colored sweat oozes between his toes, sweat of the appointed hour, sweat of a soul about to die. The Greek soldier has walked all the way from Babylon, probably has a sword, en route it becomes too much for the walking soldier, or perhaps he has discarded it, hurled it against the rocks, it could have broken in half and become buried in the earth, for the earth, it will cover all. The Greek soldier can barely drag his weary legs, the soles of his feet, are they cracked and bleeding? They came from far far far inland; sliding down mountain slopes on slender paths, through the mold of the steppes, surviving the raving winds of the ravines, the scorching heat of the craggy deserts. At one winding of the world, a dark blue light suffuses his eyes, a sparkling shimmer. The Greek soldier, all the way from Babylon, then climbed himself onto a granite outcrop, and with all his might shouted at the Black Sea: "The sea! The sea!" Had summer arrived early to the Black Sea that year, too? Before Christ?

In 1920, the fleets of the occupying forces lay anchored three-deep between Tophane and Ortaköy. A fog has descended upon the Bosporus, so thick you can't even see the water. Nearly impossible to set a course. A ship wishing to dock at Galata hugs the shore all the way from Ortaköy, skimming by mansion after mansion dotting the seaside, and even so is barely able to dock. Life was very hard at that time. At that time, too, there were wealthy citizens, shipowners, working both their ships and their crews, heirs to the sultanate, new masters of the land. The people's government wasn't yet formed, the people had yet to come to power. Three years later—1923—the government of the people that rescued the people would be established with the foundation of the Republic.

One evening I set off for the Dardanelles on the *Havran*, which was owned jointly by Sezai Bey of Edremit and Kara Vasıf Pasha. We'd taken on our cargo and passengers at the dock. And gotten our coal from a barge in front of the Tuesday Market. The gentle sound of a rueful evening *ezan* fills the decks of the enemy ships and envelops the fog. The SS *Havran*, co-owned by Sezai Bey of Edremit and Kara Vasıf Pasha, has a speed of seven and a half knots. Her steering gear isn't mechanical but operated by hand. Among the men-of-war lying at anchor we seek to wind our way. Our captain is Captain İzzet, who many years later died in the *Refah* tragedy off the shores of Cyprus when a torpedo hit the ship, and she went down with some of the navy's best submariners on board. The *ezan* has ended, Captain İzzet begins performing his prayers. I'm in the engine room. We're passing a French cruiser, heave-ho, when her underwater ram pierces our bulwark and drives into our engine shaft, into the shaft of the *Havran*, co-owned by Sezai Bey of Edremit and Kara Vasıf Pasha. But it's we who are screaming. Water begins pouring in through the gash. The current drags the ship's bow until we've broadsided the cruiser. Crying "Allah forgive me!" Captain İzzet stops his prayers, at just that moment the current pushes us free of the ram, and we begin to be dragged along by the current and to sink. It's going to take us fifteen or twenty minutes to sink, the blink of an eye. The passengers bound for the Dardanelles—men, women, and children—forget all about their sacks and their baskets, lose their patched quilts and yell and scream into the fog. Nobody wants to die. That being the case, I make a valiant effort and, with considerable assistance from third mate Tahsin, I save fifty-three passengers, putting them onto the French cruiser. It's time for the fifty-fourth, a fellow of around forty-five, he wears a tie and spectacles, has a darting gaze, a cigarette in his mouth, our eyes had met earlier on deck. It's his turn. He waits, expectantly, waving his arms, calling out to me, could it be Suphi? The ship is about to go under, and it could take me down, too, along with number fifty-four, I'm out of breath anyway, I watch him, a man in a tie, cigarette in his mouth, white shirt, yelling out, calling to me, looking left and right, running back and forth, he waves his fists at me, then at the fog, then at the ships of the occupying nations, then later at someone I cannot not make out, then he drowns along with the other fifteen passengers still on board. I watch as the water engulfs him, drowning and sinking, sinking and drowning . . . See what I've been through, so much for the nice life. Maybe it's just me, but whenever I think of that day, of that man who hung his tie in the fog . . . I think of my brother Captain Ahmet—"Who killed Suphi? Who killed Suphi?"—and that tie in the Black Sea . . .

The French lower a launch from the cruiser. Among the wreckage swirling in the current toward Seraglio Point, all they find is Captain İzzet, what's left of him from his evening prayers, clinging to a hatch. He'll go on to live until the *Refah* tragedy.

The fifty-fourth passenger doesn't live. Even though I saved fifty-three people, does the death of one man, of Suphi, make me guilty, I wonder, a traitor?

Nermin considers certain things treason, people swell, expand, and die . . . I . . . True, I wouldn't abandon home and hearth for Pola Negri's embrace. That's how my philosophy of life begins. And it changes. After the fire in Fatih, of course, I, too, had a philosophy of life, an ever-changing one. After the fire in Fatih, I started carrying my most precious possessions with me everywhere I went, but now with all my money, my mementos, my clothes buried in the sea, what was I to cling

to, what hatch was I to hang on to along with Kara Vasıf Pasha
. . . National duties, serving one's country. Board the tugboat
İhsan-ı Hüda and transport arms and ammunition to the Mim
Mim. My fountain on the banks of İkizdere had not yet run
dry, wasn't until my horse Kızbeni was shot . . .

Enough is enough! Negriyepola—like I said, truth is I was
in love with that woman. If it hadn't been for the children, I
wish I'd stayed there, rather than gone back to the bosom of a
wife mourning her fair son's death . . . What about me? After
all that I've been through? How will they remember me? Who
will? Who still knows about all that I have lived? Nermin will
change things for the better, it seems, at least leave an example
behind, a memory worthy of respect. Ha, ha, ha! Who will keep
you in mind? Who knows Nermin Hanım anyway? People
have accused even Lenin of being a traitor to his country—
yes, Lenin, your god! . . The world needs someone to blame!
If I could speak, I'd ask her now, "Nermin Hanım," Allah bids
us forget our origin—if I could only speak—come, Nermin,
my child, don't cry, don't cry, this is how Allah created people: slanting eyes, red, magenta, pink, tall, harsh, like a jellyfish crashing into a ship, its body ripped . . . To Lenin they said
in 1917, when we were in Arkhangelsk, "What are you doing,
making deals with the enemy, boarding their trains, all those
welcoming ceremonies to celebrate your arrival, where do you
think you're going with all this pomp, these Russian steppes
never birthed the likes of a muzhik like you, no, you're a spy . . ."
And if your Lenin was such a righteous man, then why didn't

he turn his guns on Ankara, that Lenin, tell them, "You killed Suphi"? Suphi who was the movement's favorite, so they said, the apple of their eye, who was killed so that Lenin might be adored... Or was Ahmet Cevat right, that he didn't even really know the first thing about communism?

So if he didn't know about it, is that why he said:

"O, world, o, you workers who are the foundation of the world, you captive peoples of the Islamic sphere, oppressed for ages, my downtrodden brothers, under foreign yokes in Egypt, Iran, India, and Turkestan, free yourselves of the torturous darkness that purchases your soul! Join the path of universal union and fraternity! O, Muslim workers of the world, my Muslim comrades crushed beneath foreign fists!

"Join together AGAINST THOSE WHO BELIEVE HUMANITY CONSISTS OF GIVING ALMS TO THE NEEDY."

That very same Ahmet Cevat who, in gratitude to his friends who declared January 28 and 29, the dates when Mustafa Suphi, Hakkı son of Hilmi, Ethem Nejat Kâzım Ali, Şefik, Gunner Hakkı, Ahmet, Yakup, Çitoğlu Nazmi, Sürmeneli, Kınalıoğlu, Aviator Hilmi, Circassian İsmail, Arab İsmail, Suphi's wife and friends—the first Turkish Communist victims—were brutally killed, days of mourning, says, "The disaster whereby fifteen Communists were mercilessly bayonetted and thrown in the sea at the shore in Trabzon is the most blatant example yet of the savagery of Turkey's bourgeois and bureaucratic class."

What was my brother going to do with Suphi's murderers anyway, was he himself a member of the Mim Mim? Suphi is said to have said himself at one point, is said to have said . . . was it he who said it, or someone else, or am I making this up? Death is at my throat, in 1913 my brother brought him to Sinop. On the *Bahricedit*, to exile in Sinop Fortress, from which Suphi escaped on a small boat across the Black Sea to Yalta, to another exile; my ship is about to go down, to be buried in the Black Sea, I rescue fifty-three passengers and place them on the French cruiser, it's the fifty-fourth passenger's turn . . . I, too, could go down along with the fifty-fourth . . . You just ask Muhafazayı Mukaddesatçı, protectors of the pious, defenders of the sultanate and the caliphate, about that . . . Ask the tradesmen and the shopkeepers, ask the Jewish merchants, ask the hodjas and the mullahs, ask the lords and the agas and the police, the pashas and the gendarmes, ask the skipper . . .

And you call me a traitor! Guilty! You're a traitor to your class, Father! Who has managed to live his life without getting mud on his face, is it you people, huh? No one's going to hand you a medal—have your fun, you're not going to fix the world. I didn't want you to suffer what I've suffered, didn't want them to use you, handle of a whip they snap in the air. That was the way I was going to take my revenge, but you wouldn't let me, I wanted you to wear furs and diamonds, to remove those overalls . . . Look at your father, no one has seen fit to decorate me, I, who . . . I, who knew how to use a machine called an indicator, who could draw a diagram of all its parts and how they worked; I was the only engineer who could diagnose just by the sound of a machine . . . Who cares about these things now? When I was in the prison camp, my captain brother looked after my wife, my life, my pipe, and my fife, if only I could sail to that ocean at Rhodes now before I die, I tell myself, if I could hop on board Hazım Peynircioğlu of Yozgat's ship, the *Hacıoğlu*, the ship he runs together with Senator Ekmekçioğlu, not too far, for my eyes have faded since they no longer see the sea, since they see nothing but the acacias and the sky, over there is a pedestal the length of the harbor, one of the seven wonders of the world, it seems to me that I, I mean we, are one of the wonders of the world, too. Me—but who's going to know? That's one of our troubles: me, those who have lived as I have. What will happen to us? What will happen to all that we have lived? Will they act as if we hadn't lived at all? Something ought to remain of so much enduring and fleeing; they say, "Everything that happens, happens for a reason," but in the end we ask was it in vain that we sailed those ships on our shoulders all those years?

The last day I asked Nermin, "Tell me, does Allah exist?" True, I'll find out for myself in a little while whether he exists or not, but, still, I thought I'd try her once more, just before dying, before setting off . . . Have you sent me on my way yet? . .

No. The ticking in this place hasn't stopped, the smell is that of my room, the hole that of the ceil— Who's that? Is it the cat? Is that the beating of my pulse leaping up to my belly, or the hum of the icebox? . .

LEYLÂ ERBİL

—

Talking to Nermin, I brought up the subject of our philosophy of life . . . I said I knew who killed Suphi: it was a Russo-English pact, also a little Greco-American league of nations, in other words, humanity, for Allah bids us forget our origin, know only that we are human beings, otherwise he brings down punishment on us, he smites our hearts. That Suphi, Suphi with his tie and his spectacles, a strange man with a darting gaze, what's he to me anyway? Let me tell you something: no matter how hard you try, Allah's will shall be done, I mean, I said, that Marx and Engels of yours, their will shall be done. I told her, I mean, if a cock crows before his time, they cut off his head— Suphi's head, I mean! . . They belittle me, they don't value me, they never have. Things happen only when the time is right, that's the way it is. I told her, Fine, in the next elections, let it be as you say, I'll vote. I stood up, leaning on my grandfather's cane—its shaft is inlaid, what hands that cane has seen, what places it's been to!—and I was off to the polls. Would you look at that! They've put me and this cane inside a room and shut the door! I searched and searched: horses, oxen, cows . . . Where are the workers? "Vote for yourself, Father! You're a laborer," urged my daughter, *laborer* is the genteel word for it, now where are those workers? . . . I'm going to vote for myself, where is my self? They've started banging loudly at the door:

—We're waiting for you, sir. May I ask what's taking so long? said a young person's voice.

158

—One minute, I'll be out in a minute.

—Come out, come out—what are you doing in there?

—What do you think, I'm looking for myself, for my picture.

—What picture?

—What do you think, a picture of a worker, there's no one in these pictures that looks like me.

And I meant it: if there'd been a picture of a fish, I'd get it, or a picture of a ferry, or a zorafina tree, but what am I to make of this? . . What kind of a man am I? I imagine myself standing before me, myself as I've been since the dress reform: a felt hat on my head, a white shirt from America, the kind that needs no ironing, a tie from Maro Cravata Kreasyon, my shoes are locally made, my feet are swollen from all the water, they won't fit in the shoes, I bend the backs of the heels and wear them like slippers, my *hutum** is well prominent now, and my *tömeçler*‡ are sticking out, my belly is swollen like the belly of a *kemençe* I've turned into a *kemençe*, the mother of the viola d'amore, which they called the chest violin, the first of which was introduced to the Istanbul palace by Nabi, who said of it, "*Yakışır sine-i Corci'ye keman*," a violin befitting the chest of Georgie, and I know how to play the *kemençe*, too, it's just like the European violin, which must have three or four chords and arrived at the Black Sea from Western Europe by way of the Genoese . . . "*Kemençe*"

---

* Adam's apple.

‡ Ribs.

is its Asiatic name, we found it floating there in the Black Sea on its swollen belly, the Greeks say "lura," the Italians "lyre," just like "*horon*" is actually "*khoron*," a dance adopted from Crimea: Caucasian, Mingrelian, Megrelian, Greek. Our origin is like that of the dance, like that of the *kemençe*, and Allah, Allah bids us forget it . . . He ascended a granite summit, a light filled his eyes, for the first time since Babylon he saw glittering water. "The sea! The sea!" he called out to the Black Sea . . . The thirty-sixth verse of the Koran in my one hand, a rapier in the other, a *kemençe* in the other, tell me already, to which nation, to which class do I belong, damn it! . .

I pressed the stamp down on a black wing. Of all of them, that must be the worker.

 —I wasn't born a worker, but you're going to kill me as one, I said to the young voice on the other side.
 —What the hell are you talking about? Get that guy out of there already . . . they cried out . . .

And I, I have emerged now and into the eighth century before, the fourth century after Christ, I am the civilization of Olivia in the work of Herodotus, *Historiarum* by Herodotus, those seas from which I emerge, into which I dive, before Mother Romrom, to the herring, to the angler, to the hermaphrodite bass, to the striped wrasse that barely swim, to the ribbonfish that look like Nermin, the robin-eyed robinfish, blue-green backs, sides of silver, bellies blackish-sparkling-purple, burrowing daytime in the bottom of the sea at the age of three, fearlessly meeting death, the *hamsi* do I ponder, none would exchange it for the riches of this world, straight into the hand of the crier, should I ask of its value, the Greek *hamsi* no less than the oxen of İpsir.

I've searched Felix, Avram, Yervant, and Devedjian's *Pêches et pêcheries en Turquie* for a picture of the *hamsi* studied by:
> the Russian Aleksandrov,
> the Russian Puzanov,
> the Romanian Treseb,
> the Finn Tikhy,
> the Turk Battalgil,
> the Greek Costa,
> the Armenian Hermin,
> the Laz Sözer,
> the Georgian Kunkut,
> the Bulgarian Shoshkov,
> the German Drensky,
> the Czech Vladikov.

Mother Romrom used to lay them out on paper, douse them in herbs ... If I'd been of the same mind as now in those days, woohoo! That Jeannine in Le Havre, a trollop after my own heart, Tamara the heathen in Constanta, frisky Calliope in Patras, Vivi, Barbara. Oh, and Sophia in Paros. Anna, Madeleine, Petkana, Monik Döla Hüsyra, Gisella Iris Sonya: Allah bids that I, that we forget our origins, like I said ... Like I said, there's something off today.

"SUPHİ! SUPHİ . . ." I shouted at the Black Sea . . .

Documents, Information, and Commentary on Mustafa Suphi

1.

I am Salih Zeki Çağatay of Trabzon. My grandfather's name was Yunus Baba. He had three sons. One of them was my father, Nuri Baba. The other two were my uncles, Mehmet and ABDÜLKADİR. My uncle Mehmet was a retired gendarme captain who passed the exams to become a trial lawyer. As a trial lawyer, he worked in partnership with Halit Özyörük in Trabzon. Among his clients was the steward of the Trabzon port, Yahya Kâhya. My other uncle, Abdülkadir, was a military veterinarian. As a captain he fell prisoner to the Russians on the Eastern front. When the revolution happened in Russia, he sided with the Bolsheviks, and he and MUSTAFA SUPHİ founded the TURKISH BOLSHEVIKS PARTY in Russia. He subsequently sent word that he and Mustafa Suphi were en route to Turkey. My uncle Mehmet showed the telegraph to Kâhya. Kâhya said that he had received a letter from Ankara that he should eradicate Mustafa Suphi and his accomplices and told my uncle Mehmet that he should abduct

A Strange Woman

my uncle Abdülkadir in order to save him. My uncle
Mehmet then went to Maçka. He met with Murat
Efendi, son of Eyüp, the kaimakam of Maçka. When
Mustafa Suphi and committee arrived in Maçka,
Murat Efendi separated my uncle Abdülkadir from the
rest of the committee. He hid him in his own home.
Mustafa Suphi and his accomplices came to Trabzon
and were eliminated in the sea, in a means and manner that are already known, by Kâhya. My uncle, who
was in hiding in Maçka, later came to Trabzon and,
with help from the Trabzon MP Hasan Saka, was
appointed to the Directorate of Veterinary Medicine
in Erzurum, and so he went there. He was later transferred to the Directorate of Veterinary Medicine in
Sivas. There, he was removed from office because of
an affair with a young woman. He went to Thrace to
practice independently as a veterinarian and settled
in Süloğlu. I have no idea what he did there. But he
stayed there for many years. He was very wealthy for a
while but then fell into poverty. The last I heard from
him was a letter dated 9.5.1957 in which he informed
me that he was still in Süloğlu and that he was living
a wretched life. We heard in 1961 that he had died in
a car crash. According to what my uncle Abdülkadir
Bey told me in my conversations with him, they left
Russia as a group of seventeen people, plus Mustafa
Suphi's wife, so a total of eighteen people. Two of
them left the group in Bayburt, my uncle himself left

in Maçka, and so, seeing as Mustafa Suphi's wife was apprehended in Trabzon, fourteen people were eradicated in the sea by Kâhya.

14 October 1967
Salih Çağatay
Former Notary Public of Trabzon and Yalova

(Mahmut Gologlu, *Cumhuriyete Doğru, 1921–1922*, Ankara, 1971, Başnur Press, p. 396)

2.

"... I remain certain today that Lenin and Stalin were opposed to both Sultan Galiev and Mustafa Suphi. Because Sultan Galiev's interpretation of Marx could have broken up Great Russia. The way to avoid this partition was to eliminate Sultan Galiev, who was responsible for producing the dynamite being laid at the foundations of Russia, and his secretary Mustafa Suphi ... There is another point we have neglected to look back upon: in 1921, we signed a treaty of brotherhood with the Russians. The exact date: 16 March 1921 ... According to one article of the treaty of brotherhood, 'Both sides agree not to recognize counterrevolutionaries' right to life.' ... Mustafa Suphi's arrival in Turkey and murder at the hands of Kâhya was in the 1920s, and the death of Sultan Galiev was around 1924 ..."

(İsmet Bozdağ, "Kemal Tahir'in Söyleşileri,"
15 June 1980, *Milliyet*)

3.

". . . Before Mustafa Suphi moved his organization to Baku, an organization called the Turkish Communist Party was established by Turks, the majority of whom were members of the Committee for Union and Progress (CUP), and this organization became engaged with the Bolsheviks. The first thing Mustafa Suphi did upon his arrival in Baku on 17 May 1920 was to disperse this party and neutralize the CUP members . . . 'Just as these individuals have no connection with us Communists, we know that they bear no relationship with Mustafa Kemal's nationalist movement either' . . . Given the Mustafa Suphi–led protests of Enver Pasha, the CUP members belonging to Enver Pasha's close circle in particular must have harbored intense animosity for Mustafa Suphi at this point . . .

"Meanwhile Talat the Little (Muşkara) and other members of the CUP, who were in Trabzon at the time, were deported in accordance with a decision

166

taken by the Grand National Assembly of Turkey...
Talat the Little may have wished to gain the confidence of Russia and get the Russians to support
Enver Pasha against Mustafa Kemal by blaming the
Ankara government for the deaths of Mustafa Suphi
and company. He furthermore may have wished to
counter in this way, before his deportation to Russia,
any accusations that might have been directed at him
regarding the aforementioned incident.

"In conclusion it may be said, though without complete certainty, that the likelihood that it was the CUP
supporters who had Mustafa Suphi and his comrades
murdered, is greater than that of other possible scenarios . . ."

(Assistant Professor Yavuz Aslan, *Türkiye Komünist
Fırkası'nın Kuruluşu ve Mustafa Suphi*, Türk Tarih
Kurumu Basımevi, Ankara, 1977)

4.

". . .The murder of Turkish Communists was carried out largely by the right-wing CUP members who had worked in Enver Pasha's Special Organization. Later Mustafa Kemal rejected Enver's request to return to Turkey via Trabzon and those men, too, were wiped out . . ."

(Andrew Mango, "Atatürk," serial, *Yeni Binyıl gazetesi*, 14 March 2000 [Sabah Kitapları]) *death*

V

The sky is clear, summer will arrive early this year, it's obvious, the sea is lucid with the light of autumn. Is that the sea? Summer will arrive early this year; the *hamsin*, the *kokolya*, the *kozkavuran*, all the winds will arrive without me.

The sky is clear, the sea is lucid with the light of autumn. Is that the Black Sea over there, will it toss me up against the shore-side mansion? . . Where am I going? In my blue pajamas—they've made me wear the bottoms as well—they are taking me away, but where to? . . What are those? Are they storks? Are the storks bleating on the green meadows? "Did you want something, Father?" If only I could speak! . . The street—this is the street, finally they are doing what they said they'd do. Or is that Galata Tower? Zorafina! Mother Romrom! She wouldn't come with us, she stayed behind, she's buried in a corner of the garden next to my father, it won't be many years before Nermin's laborers plant tea on top of them, that can't be the Eiffel Tower, the Eiffel was taller than that, the Eiffel is four-legged, Negriyepola, or is it the Bosporus, who's paved the Bosphorus with these long slabs of blue marble, why, is Mehmet the Conqueror about to pass by, or Alexander breaking his journey for a stay, is Atatürk about to pull up to the harbor and land in Samsun again, save me again, you mean Suphi, do you, or Nermin again, did we bring that marble over from Italy? Who is it that will come, that will pass this way, whoever it is on their way to liberation, they will pass, but still we are the ones who will bear the weight of the path, they will make us carry the load . . . Who's this beside me? "The road's in bad shape, I can't go any faster." "You should have taken the other road." "Too much traffic, it would have taken too long . . ." Be grateful to Menderes, for he paved this road upon which you whisk me off to death, in that case must be Üsküdar over there, the Maiden's Tower, the Maiden's Tower , , , the sky folds over, mist falls upon the sea is that the navy of the occupying forces there in front of Ortaköy ∴. .

They wouldn't kill me in my own house . . . They've paved a path of marble with broken glaze, planted a black cherry tree in the middle, dotted the surface with black seagulls . . . The ship has stopped . . . The ship has stopped, are we there , , , open the steam drains, open the exhaust valves all the way, let the steam out, loosen the steam jackets, turn on the resistors, see that the plunger bolt's in place, release the condensed water, quick, quick, turn off the drains, stop the flow, stop the leak, these men in white coats, are they the stewards , , , get them out of my engine room, which ship am I on Mother Romrom , , , that giant lid of black marble... that gaping black lid in the middle of blue marble , , , at the foot of the zorafina . . .

—

Mother Romrom! . .

Let go of me, let go of me, don't stick needles into me there, let me go, don't keep me here, the wounds of the war of independence are not yet healed, the war of independence, war of independence . . .

I don't forgive you . . . The munitions I've carried for this country , , , the bruises I've received , , , public holidays, vacation days, days of mourning , , , my horse with the white fetlocks shot and killed, Beauty Spot with the golden eyes . . . My two brothers with their golden manes who died before me , , , I don't forgive you, not for Mustafa Suphi who made the Black Sea bleed . . .

I don't forgive you for the deep scars on the soles of my feet . . . For my daughter's madness . . . For the lifetime of sweat shed on bosses' ships , , , for the fortunes they made, safe in Swiss banks , , , for the machines I looked after for fifty years, tending them like silk in cocoons , , , for the diagrams I drew of them , , , for those who came between me and my brother the captain, the doctors who couldn't identify my illness , , , I don't forgive you for the twenty-eighth and twenty-ninth of January . . .

Those who wouldn't let me die at home but dragged me to a hospital , , , who kept me waiting for death in that cold mortuary , , , who had my body washed there , , , who had me taken from there , , , who took me straight to the mosque in Şişli without letting me stop by my home , , , who buried me in this cemetery in Zincirlikuyu . . .

I forgive no one . . . no one in this world, for their sins against me. *No one. No. One. NO. ONE.*

THE MOTHER

the memorial service

We've come out of the mosque. My mother says, "Run, quickly, ask our relatives over to your house for tea, it's unseemly not to." I dash down the mosque steps and halt the departing guests. To those I'm not quick enough to stop, who are rapidly dispersing right and left, I shout: "Hey! Stop, stop, come back, come here; we have to go to my house first for some tea; my mother says so . . ." The crowd stops, and, after consulting one another, they follow me. I step quickly at first, increasing the distance between them and myself. The house is visible some 150 meters away, at the end of the street.

As I walk ahead, all alone, I scatter onto the road the candies meant to be handed out after the memorial service. The more I walk, the longer the road seems to grow, it's endless. I look behind me and see they've grown tall, very tall, that they walk in rows, four or five abreast, silent and upright. I'm frightened. The nearest row of them bends down to pick up the candies I've dropped, then straightens to follow me again. I think, since I've cast these candies for them to pick up, that they'll not do me any harm.

—

The road's wet. The water starts rising, eventually it's above my head, I begin to swim, I think they'll all drown now and I'll be free, but, looking back, I see them all swimming after me. The candies have melted away, disappeared, I start to get really frightened and I start doing the breaststroke, a stroke I know well, but suddenly the water recedes, and I find myself face-down on the ground. I get up and start to run, they catch up with me, silent and upright. As we near the house, I drag my feet, pretending to wait for them, so as not to let on that I'm afraid.

If all of them take off their shoes and their coats, it will be too much for the tiny landing at the entrance, and my mother is nowhere to be seen. What am I supposed to do with these people, what am I supposed to talk about with them? My mother was always ashamed of these relatives, and she made us feel ashamed of them as well. She never let them into her house. She'd say, "Tell them I'm not at home, that I won't be back until evening." Women like hobgoblins swathed in black. Whirling gray-blue eyes in black niqabs, sweat running out of the corners of their eyes, at their bosoms they carried small children with fine, fair hair and gray-blue eyes. "Tell her it was the mother of Uncle Zülküflü, from Kasımpaşa," they'd say. "Tell her it was Captain Hıdır's daughter-in-law," they'd say. "Well, then give your mama this hamper, my Bilal sent it to her from the old country," they'd say. Sometimes one would ask, "Which one is this?" and the other would reply, "Why, it's Hasan's woman!" Then they'd turn around and head off, hopping down the street like black insects. "Ill-mannered lot!" my mother would comment after they'd left, "Just look at them, they haven't changed one bit!" What will I talk about with them? Where will I find enough tea glasses, enough spoons? Many of the women are still veiled, and many of the men still wear green berets. They're the ones who chased us on Bloody Sunday. Whom the newspapers refer to as *the people.* Now the people are entering our house, drenched through, after all these years, let them come in, let us get acquainted. They must all be craving tea about now. Are they sad? Hard to tell. There is no emotion to read from their faces. They believe in God, now they're fulfilling their obligations toward a deceased person. The meaning of their lives is just that straightforward, just that simple. Is it really though? . .

I stand watching by the door, one end of the procession is here, the other end at the gates of the mosque, what am I to do with all these people I don't even know? . . The last person in the procession must be Meral, my sister-in-law Meral. She's handed her two-month-old baby to Menekşe, the servant girl, and is hurrying to catch up with the others. How much she's changed since getting married, she's a believer now. In God, of course. "I can't possibly leave you alone at a time like this," she says, grabbing her child and coming all the way from Sarıyer to stay with me.

—

She keeps talking about all sorts of things that I'm not the least bit interested in, toward the end I'm incapable of listening anymore. "Oh you poor dear! Your mind's wandering again, you have to let go, you do not die with the dead, you can't let your sorrow consume you," she begins. "I don't feel sorrow or anything of the sort, I'm thinking about all these realities I'd never been conscious of before . . ." I start to explain, but she doesn't understand, doesn't even listen . . . My real friends haven't come to see me at all, the ones who understand me, whom I get along with. My real friends . . . Who are they? And where are they now? When I ran into them they said, "A bunch of useless formalities . . . What does it matter . . ." But the man who died got up from his deathbed to vote, and he did that for us! What does a simple vote matter when our people are dying. What about love for the living? At a time like this, even to talk of love seems crude—things are tough, it's difficult being a leftist, it's like being a prophet, in a way. Every one of us must be a Muhammad, a Jesus, or a Moses, every single one of us; one Jesus is not enough, one Moses is not enough, it's not enough . . . What's more, these prophets, they accept you, take you in among them when you are strong of limb, but if your foot slips, if you stumble, they don't even turn to look. You may be one with them so long as you don't need them, is that it? Nothing's certain these days, nothing's decided. All values are upside down, but it will happen: someday the moral order we long for will come to be, we'll bring it about, even if it means fighting each other tooth and nail, for the very first thing we must do is get rid of the traitors amongst us, those who knowingly do wrong, who lead us astray, who deviate, we must never forgive them. Our prophethood is for the others, for those men in the green turbans . . .

I put the key in the lock and give it a turn, open the door to my people for the first time, and suddenly I notice that everything's dried off now, I see that everyone's dry. Good. Before now, it was always others who came through this door, with poems and bottles of cognac in their pockets, people constantly concerned with their own fame, I thought I understood them and that they understood me; they called upon me to reinforce their fame, to sate themselves, while I . . . Is that how it is? . . No, not quite . . .

The people are beginning to come in now, first the front row— they pass before me without looking at my face and take off their shoes. "No need to take off your shoes, Uncle, the roads weren't muddy, and there's no room for them, anyway . . ." It's as if they don't hear me, as if they're thinking, *Who are you to keep us from taking off our shoes off?* As they go in, a voice shouts their names: from Hemşin, Ismail, son of Muharrem; from Mamul, Seyfettin, Abdurrahman İslam, Hacı Salih; Temel from Vakıfkebir, Oruç, Meryem, Akife, Zehra; my father's relatives from the province of Çayeli, Captain Bilal, Skipper Ali, Aunt Hafize; the clan from Bilginol, the İshakoğulları, Behzatoğulları, Sabitoğulları, Kibaroğulları, Aunt Zehra.

Bekir, my father's dentist, and his wife—them I know—the members of his crew, Recep, Salih, Rüfet, Ramazan; Dr. Naci, who properly diagnosed my father's illness, and his mother—I know them too—Melek Hanım, Mürüvvet Hanım, and Captain Tahsin—I know him. Şaban from Sürmene; Mustafa Yazıcıoğlu and his children from Maçka; Necmettin Molla, Sahure Hanım, and Captain Rahmi . . . Coming out of the hospital, a man slipped a thick envelope into my hands, a package. "This is yours," he said. When I looked into the envelope, I recognized the teeth; I recognized the bright pink gums: "I forgive no one, no one!"—Aunt Safiye; Rıza the Foreman; Yusuf, father's favorite—they went hunting together—and his sons, Selami, Asım, and Ömer. All three with their hawks on their arms, the hawks all scrunched up, round like little pitchers, sleeping, their eyes shut. Uncle Yusuf has placed the large sack on his back in the middle of the room, a sack that wriggles—my father would return with a bunch of quail, tell my mother, "Here take these, they're enough for a small bottle of rakı, they've probably escaped from Russia"—the sons of father's uncle: Captain Ziya, Aunt Asiye, their sons-in-law, Chipper Ahmet and Sweetie Musa—I know Musa, he used to put me on the back of Walnut Ali; Walnut Ali was the name of that big white stork, it would rise, carrying me into the air, and then bring me back down. Hadiyanım, the daughter of Zero Hasan Pasha; the daughter of my father's uncle; her sons, Zeki and Hasan; her daughters-in-law, Rakibe Abla and Hatçe Abla; Esma; Hızır; Dursun; Osman Gavras from Yomra, or rather, Vona, the one who wrote the folk song about

İsmail of Soytaro: "Oh, no, Soytaro, seized and killed / With your blood the station is filled. / The major, that scoundrel, he did this to you / Because the Turkish people, they recognized you." Hüseyin, Yunus, Bangoğulları, Hilmi and İhsan—my friends from the party—Meral, Menekşe, and the baby. And my mother's here, too. I ask the voice, "Are none of the ship-owners here?" and it replies, "Not one." "Fifty years, easier said than done, he gave them fifty years of his life," I insist. "Not one of them has come," the voice repeats. "Anyway, they don't stay in Turkey this time of year: schools are on holiday, they go to see their children in Europe, they go skiing, they go shopping, you know that," it says. "Yes, I do," I say, and I shut the door.

Menekşe puts the baby on the floor, my mother appears, "Did they all fit?" she asks. "I don't know. I suppose so," I say. I call to the woman in the kitchen, "Şirin, make one hundred glasses of tea." "What do you mean *tea*?" my mother shouts. "Are you throwing a party on the day of your father's memorial service?" "But you said to!" I snap. Suddenly she's breaks down sobbing. "Don't cry, Father's here with us, too," I plead, and she stops. "Where is he, show him to me," she says. I show her the sack twitching on the floor. "Don't tell anyone he's here or they'll run away," she says. She looks at the multitude that fills the house, "I told you to invite our relatives!" she yells at me, then turns to them: "If you aren't a relative, leave now!" When no one moves she continues, "Hey, didn't you hear me, I said if you're not a relative, get out!" "Scandalous!" Hüsniyanım huffs at my mother. "First they invite us and then they drive us away." My mother grabs her by the collar and drags her to the door, then runs back inside. "Go on, go on, hurry up now!" she orders, kicking the neighbors out. "Mother, don't be rude, let them be," I say. "No, no, let them all go to hell, I don't want to see them," she says. "When you were a girl, they gossiped about you something awful." "Forget about all that now," I say. "No, why should I, I don't want to forgive those who do evil, I haven't even forgiven your father, not in my heart, let alone Mürüvvet Hanım. She used to strip bare all the flowers your father planted. How your poor father loved those lilac bushes, he never had a chance to properly enjoy their fragrance, she used to steal the blossoms at night, when we were asleep, the thieving creature!" The women stand up, muttering, and begin to leave. "This woman's crazy!" they say. "And anyway," my mother continues, "with the cost of living what it is, it's not as if we're getting tea and sugar for free, let them drink tea in their own houses!" "Please forgive her, she's not herself," I say, but my mother snarls, "I am, I am myself, now will you stop fawning over these shrews." "Talk about shameless," says Mürüvvet Hanım angrily, "as if we're in it for the tea. First they make us listen to the birth song in an ice-cold mosque, make us say all the prayers and all the amens, then they shoo us away, God willing that man will twist and turn in agony in his grave!" My mother brings her handbag down on the woman's face, a few of us try to restrain her, we separate them, show the woman the door. This time my mother runs up to Melek Hanım. "Come on, out with you, too, you two-faced convert," she says. "Mother," I say, taking hold of her hands, "you are being so rude, what are you doing?" "Let me be, let me give a piece of my mind to this greedy noblewoman, unworthy wife of the military attaché, ha, and here I thought she was decent, turns out all this time she's been calling us 'dirty Laz' behind our backs, says we changed the smell of the neighborhood, that our place reeks of cooking grease so badly she can't bear to walk by our front door, aha, there's Esma Hanım, let her tell you herself . . ." Melek Hanım stands up, saying, "Good heavens, what boorish manners." "Go on with you, you Salonica Jewess, you two-faced . . ." my mother says, chasing her away. "Now you sit down, Esma dear, I won't let you go—Naci, too, he's not going either, we'll have some tea together . . ." she says, then she sits down herself, muttering, "Look at that hussy, would you, saying we changed the smell of the neighborhood, why, you came to the neighborhood after us, and you never cook, so of course your house never smells of grease! Woe is me! My poor, poor husband, he should have had some of my mashed black cabbage one last time, he wanted it so, but the doctor wouldn't let him have it, or anything else for that matter, the rotten swine, they starved my husband, that mountain of a man, to death, made him dwindle down to nothing . . ." She runs up to the door and slams it shut behind the last of them. "That's it, let's stay here among ourselves, we of the same flesh and blood—scorpions wouldn't do the damage to each other that relatives do," she says.

The relatives have filled the living room and the adjoining room. The children sit cross-legged, the young stand crowded together, most of the men have prayer beads in their hands, the women's heads are bowed, their eyes fixed on the floor. Meral's baby suddenly gets out of its swaddling clothes, climbs onto the piano stark naked, and jumps up and down on the lid. Meryem, pointing at the piano, asks, "Oh, what's this?" "A piano," I reply. "What do you do with it?" "You play it." İhsan approaches it and with one finger plunks the melody of the "Tenth Anniversary March." Protests of "La-İllahi-illallah" rise from the crowd, but İhsan continues: "Led by a man the world respects." The young gather around the piano and begin to sway, the baby begins to quiver from head to toe doing new dances, and the others follow suit; Meral claps her hands in rhythm and shouts, "Well done, my little girl, shake, shake, shake . . ." İhsan leaves the piano and mingles with the dancers, he, too, begins to writhe, as though in the throes of death; the piano repeats the tune, over and over, all by itself: "Led by a man the world respects . . . Led by a man the world respects . . ." "I forgive no one, no one!" They all writhe in unison.

"My girl, who is this?" Abdurrahman asks, pointing at a picture on the wall with the hand in which he holds his prayer beads, "Your father-in-law, is it?" "No, Uncle, that's one of our writers." "Our what, our what?" Hilmi comes to my aid, explaining, "Uncle, that's a great Turkish writer." "Never heard his name before," observes Abdurrahman, my mother appears. "Were you asking about that man, Uncle Abdurrahman? Oh, if you only knew! Such a wealthy man, asked for the hand of my daughter, but I refused him, if I'd given her to him she'd own *han*s and hammams now. Oh, what an idiot what a block-head I am, I gave her to that pipe-smoking pig instead, and he's destroyed my little girl, made her sick . . ." Aunt Hafize eyes me, "What, you mean this here lass is sick?" "She certainly is, Auntie, she's mad, absolutely mad!" my mother says. "Her husband's driven her mad. Do you know what he does, Auntie? When they're alone in the evening, when everyone else has left, he pulls up a chair facing her and sits there for hours, staring at her, silent, 'Please, say something!' my daughter begs, and the guy still doesn't speak, just goes on staring at her, without blinking an eye; then suddenly he begins to shout, 'Mad, mad, mad, mad as a hatter.' He repeats this a thousand times, every evening—unbelievable, I know, but I swear it's the truth, Aunt Hafize, I watched them secretly one night, and I heard it with my own ears, may I die unwashed if I'm lying! . ." "Well, the poor wretch, why didn't you tell me she has nowhere to go," clucks Aunt Hafize. Captain Bilal: "Where's this son-in-law of yours now, is he here?" "As if! An unbeliever like him at a memorial service? Woe is me, Captain, woe is me! If I had but a single sorrow, how easily the tears would flow," says my mother, then in a whisper, "He thinks he's God himself." "Oooh, what are you saying, Allah forbid!" they gasp. "He wasn't that far gone at first, but after he saw his father die, he lost his mind completely." "Oooh, what are you saying?" "He's like some kind of bogeyman, wandering the streets at night, pacing up and down his house, going on and on about how he's going to save everyone, saying, 'I am your good Allah, I will free you from that evil Allah, from all your ills,' till he's thoroughly lost his mind . . ." The piano keeps on playing the same tune again and again: "Led by a man the—" "I forgive no one, no one!"

Aunt Safiye asks about another picture on the wall. "He's also a great man," I answer. "What's his name?" "Ilyich." "Is he an infidel?" "Yes." "What's he to us, then?" Hilmi cuts in, "Auntie, he was a very, very great man, he saved his country, its workers . . ." They stand up, each of them pointing at a picture. "Ah, who's this one?" "Who's that one?" "Here, here, who's this here?" "He conquered the enemy . . . Capitalism and imperialism . . . The poor . . ." "You mean a comunis, you mean a comunis . . ." they say rousing one another. "We've already heard plenty of things about this girl, come on, get up, be careful not to touch anything in this house or you'll be defiled, have to do your ablutions all over again, 'cause you'll be defiled . . ." "Look here, you scorpions," warns my mother, "you shut your mouths, no one can speak ill of my daughter as long as I'm alive, I'm her mother and her father both; you wouldn't know a comunis if you saw one, you jackals, now don't get me started!" And she grabs Emrullah by the collar. "You, you old ghoul—you already made life hard enough for me in the past, and my husband was miserable when he passed all because of you, and now this, too, is your doing, I know it," she says, hurling him against the wall. "Get up! Get up, don't drink the tea these people make! Oh, we've been defiled!" they are shouting, jostling one another, when my mother stops Necmettin Molla, "And you, of all people, how quickly you've forgotten that bastard your daughter gave birth to, knocked up by your chauffeur, I shit on your beard, you pimp! . ." she says yanking roughly at his beard. Rüfet drives his fist into Castro's face, and the others, seeing this, attack the other picture frames; they knock down wall plates, tear apart my oil paintings, my Nuri İyem, my Levni, my Fahir Aksoy, my Avni Memetoğlu. "You think, *Oh, he's dead now*, and so we've been left without a man forevermore, don't you? Well, I'll cut you down to size, I will!" my mother says and runs into the bedroom, picks up the wriggling sack and hoists it over her shoulder, brings it in, and unties it. Thousands of birds burst out: quail, pintail duck, plover, woodcock, fieldfare, crested lark, partridge. They fill the air. Wild duck, ruffled grouse, guinea fowl, sandgrouse, pintail duck flutter above our heads. The hawks drowsing on the arms of Selami, Asım, and Ömer go wild and give chase, the dancers open their arms and legs wide and scream as they twirl about on the floor. "Led by a man the world respects." "I forgive no one, no one!" Hadji Salih, Recep Temel, Molla, the Sofuoğlus all attack me. Meral, Captain Sabri, Hilmi Musa, Chipper Ahmet protect me, my mother bellows, "Where's your father, where's your father?" as she searches the sack. Not finding him, she sinks to the floor, her face waxen.

I pull at İhsan's arm, give it a shake: "Wake up, wake up! The way you're dancing, it's unseemly. Help us. Can't you see what's happening?!" İhsan stops dancing and pulls a Molotov cocktail out of his pocket. "Don't you dare, you idiot. You throw that, and you'll wipe us all out," I say. Then I continue, my voice somewhere between a roar and a moan, a moan and an entreaty, "Stop, listen to me, my brothers and sisters, my elders: stop, don't shed blood in vain, *you* are people who know God; abandon anger and evil, we're all of the same blood, come, let's all hold hands, come let me save you, I'll be your good Allah, follow me . . ." Someone brings his fist down on my back. "Shame on you! You godless woman, *you* are going to be a prophet to us? Repent, repent!" they all begin shouting . . . "She's not one of us, she can't possibly be of our blood; her father was strange, too: the first to wear a hat, first to make his wife wear a hat, first to send his daughter to school, he only went to mosque on the Bayram holidays, and even then he never wore a kufi!" Temel has Hilmi on the ground and is kicking at him; someone else has gripped a tuft of Chipper Ahmet's hair and is dragging him along the floor; Yazıcıoğlu has cornered Musa and is punching him in the nose; Musa keeps shouting, "Walnut Ali, Walnut Ali!" I run to my room, grab the ceremonial sword passed down from my grandfather, and brandish it at them. "You deserve to have your blood spilled, you're asking for it," I yell, martyring several of them. "You understand nothing of prophethood," I say. "Death is your just deserts, death . . ." I chase the enemy. Those not fighting watch us, clapping, while those fleeing scramble to get out the door, leaving their shoes behind at the entrance.

Out the open door fly the birds, followed by the hawks. My mother comes up and kisses me. "Like I said, I have no son but, you are both my son and my daughter, both my son and my daughter." She's weeping. My father grows quiet now, too. He doesn't say "I forgive you," though, and he shouldn't.

The sword is in my hand. I turn to those who have abstained from the fight and say, "Off you go, or else I'll send your heads flying, too." They also run away. Meral wipes the sweat off my brow, then she and Şirin gather the broken glass and tidy the room. All of us who fought on my side are hugging and kissing each other. "What about the dead?" I ask. "They've taken their dead with them," they reply. The doorbell rings, my husband comes in and kisses me on the cheek, asking, "How are you, my darling?" "Where were you?" I snap. "You should be ashamed of yourself." The smell of rakı is in the air. "Oh, gosh, sorry—I forgot about the service, I only remembered it just now," he says. "What the hell happened to this place?" "We fought a war, a war, we fought without a single man to help us, and we won!" my mother, says. "You people are mad," my husband guffaws. "You're the one who's mad!" I fire back, and we all laugh. The piano continues to play itself, "Led by a man . . .". "Shut that thing up!" I shout to İhsan. He gives it a good kick, the baby comes down and gets back into its swaddling clothes, the dancers come to their senses. İhsan begins to plunk with one finger again: "Sit down, my love, sit down, upon the pier of Rize / The woes of my heart I cannot say." "Now you can bring the tea!" I tell Şirin. "And you can have all those shoes, too." "Very well, miss," Şirin replies, happy as can be. We all dance the *horon* together.

THE WOMAN

Bayan Nermin, ten years a member of the Labor Party, had just finished skiing. She opened the window of her room and looked onto the mountainside opposite. The sun spread a pinkish-purple haze across the darkened slopes. Flakes descended, thick and sparse. A few spruce trees jutted out here and there; they appeared to be imploring nature, their heads bowed to bear the weight of the snow that was their allotment, arms dangling low. Bayan Nermin took in a long breath of that nature, drawing it into the very depths of her lungs, and as she let it out the sound of voices filled her ears: "Look at that guy, he's putting a belt around her ass!" Bayan Nermin looked in the direction of the sound. It was two village boys. They stood watching the crowd of men, women, and children waiting to ride the lift to the top of the mountain, ski down the slope as fast as they could, then ride up again. Both boys had their hands in their pockets, their shoulders drawn in, their chins flattened. Every time the lift started, they leapt into the air, releasing to the ground the snow that had clung to them, and making bestial sounds, apparently of joy.

Bayan Nermin threw herself onto the hotel room's sofa, still in her ski clothes. Something like tenderness crossed her face.

"Someday, perhaps they, too . . ." she mused aloud, but then interrupted herself, "Not supposed to think about that, no no no no no."

Bayan Nermin had joined the party as soon as it was founded. It seemed to her at the time that in no more than three, four years her working-class brethren would descend upon the city squares en masse, in numbers too great to be contained—though admittedly these squares were no bigger than the palm of one's hand—their shouts would pierce the tinseled sky, and the long-awaited society "free of class, rid of privilege" would burst into being. That this was no easy task became evident in the very first days, but Bayan Nermin took all difficulties in stride; it came naturally to her. The most important thing now, as it had been then, was to "go down to the people," to quote the party president. Bayan Nermin knew what party discipline meant. Indeed, she was among those who for years had waited to be educated with such discipline. She shuddered slightly when she heard the phrase *down to the people* but didn't say anything. Only deep inside she thought, *They mean "reach the people, rise to the people."* Yes, in this sense, one could only "rise." What had begun with talks, meetings, discussions, was soon followed by marches, chases, escapes, and bruises from sticks and stones. But Bayan Nermin had no intention of conceding defeat or disillusionment. In spite of all the evil forces at work, she knew that one day the people would come to understand them, and they, the people. In fact, they were already under the impression that they understood the people, though for some reason they couldn't seem to make this clear to the people.

On those days when they went in groups to visit the shantytowns, once they began to explain to the inhabitants how they'd been hoodwinked, a few of the people would emerge from behind the front row of attentive listeners to throw rocks and stones at their heads, at which point the previously passive attendants in the front rows, who had just been listening attentively with hopeful glints in their eyes, would rise like a wave and begin shouting with the others, "Go back to Moscow, go back to Moscow!"

Bayan Nermin returned home on such days with a burning heart and discussed the events with her husband as she pondered other ways of rising to the people, this unwary people, a people deceived—but only because it was as pure as angels, and as naive as the mentally ill.

It was as though they enjoyed torturing themselves, thought it virtuous to suffer and so refused to free themselves from the ordeals they had endured for centuries, while Bayan Nermin's own ordeal was a twinge of doubt that perhaps she was incapable of understanding this saintly people of hers, and she suffered the ordeal of this doubt as if she, too, were part of her people. Still she believed that there must be a way to penetrate the layers and layers, the strata of petrified shells that had encapsulated her people. It did not escape her attention that the greater the difficulties she encountered, the more her passion grew. "Have I chosen this path because I love my people," she wondered, "or is it my anger toward the others that drives me?" But she also knew that finding the answer to this question was of no importance. What mattered now was that she remain firmly on the path she had chosen, whatever the reason for her choice, and that she could proclaim, before she died, "Mission achieved."

Bayan Nermin and her husband were enlightened people. Though he may not have shared her views, her husband was understanding and, as time went on, increasingly supportive. Bayan Nermin carefully thought the matter over, discussed it at length with her husband, and finally persuaded Bay Bedri that in order for her to fulfill her obstinate desire to get to know the people, they had to move their home from the smart neighborhood of Osmanbey to the shantytown of Taşlıtarla. Her husband refused, however, to change his place of work. By all means, let his wife offer her services to the "scroungers" of Taşlıtarla if she must, "but, please, I beg of you," she was not to interfere in his professional life.

On a cloudless May morning, just as the bellflowers and tickle grass were beginning to sprout here and there, she sold for a song to the neighborhood's Kurdish rag-and-bone man the rosewood bedroom and the three-piece living room suites that had been part of her dowry, while her sideboard and glass cabinet she installed in her mother's dining room, and to her mother she also entrusted her silver, saved for a rainy day, and then she had sufficient furniture for the two-room shack she'd rented in Taşlıtarla loaded onto a truck. As the mother's eyes gazed tearfully at this foolish daughter who had been a handful from her youngest days, silently she prayed, "God grant her reason, whatever shall I say to the neighbors, please God, let me see the day when this daughter of mine now approaching forty finally comes to her senses, else I will not die in peace." To her daughter, she said, "So you're deserting me, when I've already got one foot in the grave, well the least you can do is stay away from here for a while so I can tell my friends you've taken a trip to Paris." Annoyed Bayan Nermin shot back, "Oh, those awful friends of yours, and to think you're still trying so hard to impress them!" then she embraced her mother and kissed her wrinkled cheeks. "Well, keep your spirits up, I won't come by for a while. You can tell them I've gone off to America to do some shopping, if you like," she said, hugging her mother, and then she left. To be sure the journey was auspicious, her mother flung the contents of a glass of water onto the front step, taking care not to wet the doormat.

Bayan Nermin saw to it that her rubber wood reading chair was placed high on the load in the truck, then she plopped herself down on it, crossed her legs, and lit a cigarette. She was on her way to Taşlıtarla.

As the truck took off, she couldn't repress the urge to make a gesture from childhood, one more common to boys, signifying

"So much for you!" toward the apartment she'd just vacated, but then she just as quickly sank back into herself, scanning the surroundings with fearful eyes to make sure she hadn't been observed. Recalling all the times she'd been slapped by her mother for making this gesture, she smiled.

She choked with happiness throughout the journey, and, to calm herself, a little at least, she sang as loudly as she could. She heard that her throat had suddenly cleared and her voice had begun to ring out smooth and warm. The truth is, Bayan Nermin had never harbored any superstitions, but she understood from the beauty of her new voice that she was experiencing a kind of spiritual exaltation. It was a level of emotion attained only by those who unselfishly dedicated themselves to serving their society, their people. She wished her mother could hear this new voice.

She rose to her feet and looked at the sky, at that open space quickly filling up with herringbone cuts of darkness, now and then she fell back down when the truck shook, but she pulled herself up, and would fall again, and rise again, listening with damp eyes to the sound of her voice, which became emphatically more beautiful with each rise and fall.

Her feelings turned from joy to apprehension, from apprehension to fear, from fear to exuberance, and each time she saw people she opened her arms and greeted them lovingly. If she'd dared, she would have blown them kisses, done a belly dance. She did not, but she did occasionally cry out loudly enough for them to hear, "Together, all together!" People stopped to gaze at the truck and smile in astonishment, before continuing along their way. Bayan Nermin interrupted her song only to begin again, over and over; she listened to hear if her voice was still as beautiful as before, and once she was certain of its beauty, she resumed waving to the people. She became breathless, and another voice from within her rang out: "How grateful I am, how grateful I am to my people—who are neither man nor beast, neither cunning nor dumb, who neither love nor are loved, but for whom my love has wrenched me away from the bourgeoisie, the miscreated, rotten-hearted bourgeoisie who found fault with even my most innocent acts!" Then she would clap and begin singing again.

When she finally reached her new home, nearly faint, she jumped from the truck and, as she always did when in a pinch, ran her left fist over her teeth. Back in the old home there was still a piano: she hadn't been able to decide whether to sell it. She went back and forth in her mind. The piano occupied a special place in her life. A separate, fragmented, magical place. It symbolized the past and the fragmentation of Bayan Nermin, it was a monument to the errors of a nation, the crimes of a family. She thought, by turns, of how her mother, saving and stinting in their most difficult days, had nevertheless insisted on piano lessons for her from a White Russian teacher popular at the time; how on the days when she had get-togethers at home with neighborhood ladies, she would push Nermin forward, saying, "Go on, play some Chopin for us"; how she herself had fallen in love with the White Russian monsieur; how the two of them had kissed; how one day when they were kissing, her mother had rushed out of the bathroom, and, not even pausing to cover her private parts, had chased him away saying, "I'll show you a Tatar bride's instrument right about now," and flung a bar of soap at the thick-necked, blond dolichocephalic, leaving a welt on top; how she'd then turned around and given her daughter a sound beating, screaming, and for years had lamented, "With a heathen to boot! A heathen!"; and how she had kept this a secret from Nermin's father and thus maintained her monopoly on authority. Bayan Nermin pulled her fist away from her teeth. "Seeing as such an instrument exists in the world, it would do my people good to know of it," she thought, and when the truck was unloaded, she sent it back for the piano.

The first problem of her new life thus presented itself: the R. Erblich und Söhne grand piano wouldn't fit through the front door of the shanty. It was getting dark. Once more, Bayan Nermin pressed her fist against her teeth and, uttering, "Anything for the people," had the instrument installed under a stunted plum tree in the yard. That day, for the children of Taşlıtarla—who were speechless as they watched the black monster it had taken eight movers to load and unload, with some removing and replacing of bits and pieces here and there—life suddenly became surreal. Their arms akimbo, like their fathers', their heads bunched together in little groups as they pretended not to look at the black bird, and Bayan Nermin, her voice shaking with emotion, called to her side these lovable children with their small necks, bulging eyes, and crooked legs. The children turned and looked the other way. The roughest among them, though, with brows knitted and one hand in his pocket, approached her with slow steps, and the others soon followed. "Well, children, this musical instrument is what they call a piano. Let me tell you about it. You see, this instrument first appeared in the eighteenth century. But it's not one of our instruments. Every country has instruments of its own, born of its history. For instance, the Swiss are a nation of shepherds. Their musical instrument is like a giant *kaval*, but so long that when one end is in your mouth, the other end would reach, say, to that pomegranate tree over there. Now, our instruments are different: we have the *kaval*, and also the bagpipes, the lute, the *kemençe*, the oud, the zither . . ." Bayan Nermin explained, beginning her lesson.

The children appeared not to understand, or not to be listening, and they continued staring at her with knitted brows. "Come closer," Bayan Nerim smiled. "I'll play it for you, and you'll hear the sound it makes." She grabbed a chair, announced, "A waltz by Chopin," and began to play. When she stopped, she turned to find the garden filled with men, women, and children. One little girl had tried to dance to the music, but her mother had put an end to this with a blow to her back. With a burst of heartfelt laughter Bayan Nermin shouted "Hello!" to the people. They murmured back, "Hello." Then the men slowly withdrew, and the women, after a shock, said, "Welcome." Some of them silently followed the men, a few remained behind, remarking, "May you live happily in your new home," "How are you, then," and the like. Bayan Nermin repeated her lecture for their benefit and added that, if they wished, she could give piano lessons to their children. To this the women gave no reply but merely looked at each other. This pleased Bayan Nermin. She realized that she had behaved before with unnecessary exuberance, as though under the influence of some fear. The offer of piano lessons, alongside the instilling of class consciousness in the people, would be met with derision by members of the party, that much she knew. And so to herself once more she lovingly embraced the people, who protected her from this. "Eh, you settle in a bit, and we'll come to see you," the women promised, holding their veils with their teeth as they walked away. "My dear, dear people!" Bayan Nermin said. To herself she vowed to be calmer in the future, not to be so emotional, not to act so rashly. *Much of what I did today was wrong,* she chided herself.

Bayan Nermin's husband, Bay Bedri, came home from work early that evening. After driving around and around for some time in search of a place to park his Impala, he finally managed, with the help of one of their new neighbors, to find a spot a five-minute walk from the house. The neighborhood, adults and children alike, did not exhibit for the car the same interest they had for the grand piano. Only a few children, more curious about the driver than the car, ran after it, waiting for this new person to get out, and then accompanied him to his home.

—

Bayan Nermin met her husband at the gate of their small garden. It was dark now, they went straight inside, and shared a long kiss. While Bay Bedri filled his pipe, Bayan Nermin related the day's events to him. They wouldn't find the place too odd; he should imagine he'd gotten a job with the United Nations, and they'd been assigned, for instance, to the Congo. Hadn't Bay Bedri filled out countless applications, and wasn't he still awaiting a favorable reply? Well, this place probably couldn't be any worse than whatever they might encounter in that scenario. "Yes, darling," agreed Bay Bedri, "but I'd be earning two thousand dollars there, let's see that I don't spend more than that here." Still, he seemed quite content.

Within a few months of moving to Taşlıtarla, Bayan Nermin grew accustomed to her new surroundings. She was, after all, a highly adaptable person. Furthermore, she was engaged in a struggle for a better understanding of the people. In these complicated days, at this great juncture, it would be nothing less than base for her to even to think of the petty bourgeois inclinations of her past. Taşlıtarla wasn't nearly as bad a place as it was said to be. Its inhabitants were quiet. They appeared to get along with each other. From time to time there'd be a quarrel, due, often as not, to the children, but the resulting sulkiness didn't last more than a day or two. Neighbors visited one another frequently. She, too, had visitors. The neighbors did their research about Bayan Nermin. And they undertook this research openly to her face: Who was her father, her mother? What did they do for a living? Were they alive? How much did they earn? Did they own their house? Her mother-in-law, her father-in-law, her brothers- and sisters-in-law, their jobs, their monthly earnings, did they own a washing machine? How many children did each of them have? Why didn't Bayan Nermin have any children? And most important of all, where was she, where was her family REALLY from? If the family owned a house, why didn't mother, daughter-in-law, and father-in-law all live together, why had she and her husband come here to live? While living among the others, Bayan Nermin would have thought such curiosity vulgar. She could not have helped but mock such curiosity about one's origins, one's income, when expressed by those gentlepeople. But the interest exhibited openly now by her people did not annoy her at all, she patiently answered each and every query. And when she understood that they had run out of questions, Bayan Nermin plunged into an explanation of the system, the difference between this system and others, of how they belonged to a society composed of classes. The women listened with evident restlessness, they tried to change the subject, they didn't seem to understand what she was saying, sometimes not ten minutes would have passed before they rose to leave—"Eh, time we be going, it's getting late"—and walked out. There was such a vast emptiness to their movements, in the looks in their eyes, in the way they sat, that Bayan Nermin found herself unable to continue speaking. It was as though as soon as she opened her mouth, the conversation was already over. That was how they behaved. Bayan Nermin had thought progress would be slow, but that she should be stopped in her tracks in this manner frightened her. There must, there absolutely must, be another, easier way to dispel the mistrust that had accumulated in them over the centuries and convince them that the socialists were different, that they were not after personal gain at all.

Bay Bedri was devoted to his wife. From the very beginning he felt an admiration for her childlike sincerity. The loftiness of her aims in dragging him into this mess buttressed his admiration with respect. The same respect was awakened in Bayan Nermin's party friends, too. During the long summer evenings, a group of them, men and women both, took to dropping in more and more frequently, they would gather around the table, always set and waiting under the acacia tree just beyond the piano, and sometimes remain there until daybreak, eating, drinking, and talking politics. Though invited, the neighbors did not participate in such gatherings. Local party members Rıza, a printer, and a young man in his second year at law school, who lived next door, would occasionally and silently join them, sip their rakı, and shyly help themselves to the food on the table, then early on ask for permission to leave without having taken part in the discussions.

One evening the party chairman himself turned up. He courteously shook hands, inquired after each person there, and then asked for information about the neighborhood. With some embarrassment, Bayan Nermin explained that the people here

LEYLÂ ERBİL

seemed satisfied with their lives, that they didn't wish anything changed, and that the lot of them were in favor of the
party presently in power. The chairman listened, and, in the
voice of someone on a visit of condolence, urged her not to
be disheartened, not to be taken in by appearances, said that
it wasn't possible to predict what the people would do, or
when they would do it, and advised her to be patient and continue educating them. Turning to look at the grapevine, riddled with phylloxera, which clung to a few twisted sticks at one
end of the garden, he talked of the production of grapes, of
middlemen, and again of the education of the people. "What
a beautiful garden, what a beautiful place," he observed. "But
our people will create more beautiful places and make them
thrive," he went on. "In this struggle for independence, our
people will conquer their enemies, internal and external." At
that moment Bay Bedri removed his pipe from his mouth and,
turning toward the chairman, "Sir," he began, "this same people won their first war of independence, but we see here the
net result of their victory. What I mean to say is, what sense
is there in making the people struggle for their independence
again and again if victory is to be followed by this?" Everyone
listened to these words in stunned amazement, having no idea
what to make of them . . . After her husband, who took no particular interest in such political issues and certainly took no
part in efforts around them, had made his messy pronounce-
ment, Bayan Nermin could only exclaim, "How dare you!"
The chairman, however, responded, "It is not us but objec-
tive conditions that have forced the people into this second

struggle for independence. It's quite impossible to force the people to do something they don't want to do! Furthermore, all struggles don't necessarily end in the same way, I should say." This mature behavior on the part of the chairman on this occasion endeared him to all present. Bay Bedri emptied his pipe, refilled it, and began noisily puffing at it. The subject was changed, and they talked of the unnatural heat that summer, of the tour of the provinces due to begin next month, and of the latest American missile launch. Then the chairman rose and asked for the hosts' permission to leave. Talât, Muzaffer, İhsan, and Osman stood up with him. Bayan Nermin and her husband accompanied the chairman to the nearest taxi stand. It was a silent walk, save for replies to the chairman's questions:

"This must be a private house, sir."

"Over there, you mean—it's a police station."

"Yes, it's quite a large building, it's the headquarters of the Society for the Struggle Against Communism, sir."

The sound of the footsteps of these six people walking in the dark seemed to rise from the rough cobblestones and echo upon Bayan Nermin. On parting, the chairman shook their hands warmly, holding them in his grasp for several moments. "I congratulate you," he said, turning to Bayan Nermin, "and wish you success."

She didn't take her husband's arm on the way back. When they arrived home, she went straight to bed without a word and proceeded to open Politzer's book on the philosophy of

Marxism and commence reading. Bay Bedri lingered in the yard, lit his pipe, looked through the papers, and turned out the lights. When he came to bed, he found his wife already asleep. Politzer's book lay between Bayan Nermin's breasts.

Turning from one side to the other on the hotel sofa, she moaned, "No, no, I don't regret anything, I don't, these things had to happen." She got up and paced back and forth for a bit, she could feel the pain softly stirring within her, sensed it was making its way from the voids within to her stomach. "I won't think," she said. "I'll do what the doctor told me." What the doctor had told her was "Take a journey, go back to nature, don't do any serious work, get some exercise, keep yourself amused. In fact," he had said, "do exactly as you wish, don't put any pressure on yourself!" Bayan Nermin had averted her eyes from those of the doctor, who scrutinized her from every angle as he spoke these words; she made a dash for her purse, paid his fee, and thanked him as she ran out.

She leaned out the window again and looked down. The two children below shook their faces, beet-red from the cold, right and left, they blew on their hands, making awkward movements as they kicked back like agitated horses. The skiers in their multicolored rainproof jackets raced down to the valley and back in straight lines, fell and picked themselves up in orderly fashion, forming a constant colorful line up and down the slopes. It was as though those two children were the dwarf clowns of this snow circus. She felt an uncontrollable anger spreading through the cells of her body, and, as it spread, the pain in her stomach grew. Unconsciously, she began to pace quickly around the room. She recalled the argument with her husband. "You should take yourself to a psychiatrist; your hatred of anyone who isn't poor or in pain may be the result not of revolutionary ardor but rather of pathological disease," Bay Bedri had said one Sunday. Bayan Nermin could scarcely believe her ears. The conversation continued:

"The simplest name for this disease is a little conscience combined with a little common sense!"

"If you truly believe that the working class is to be saved by the bourgeois likes of you, or the likes of us, then by all means go on with your little game, enlighten your people . . ."

"I wasn't aware that you were engaged in this field of study."

"What field?"

"Reading books, research."

"In other words, you would deprive those who don't carry a book under their arm of the right to speak!"

"What I know is that intellectuals are, and can be, leaders in this struggle."

"Why can't you be realistic? This isn't China, it's another country altogether. The only reason I've kept quiet all this time is because I respect everyone's right to freedom of belief. But if you think I believe that the gap caused by centuries can be closed by spending a year or two in Taşlıtarla, then you must be very naive indeed."

"And you'd like that gap to close without the intellectuals risking so much as a nosebleed!"

Telling herself once again, "I mustn't think," Bayan Nermin ceased pacing the room. She looked out at the thin pink slice that remained of the sun. She took out her camera, aimed it at the sun, focused, and snapped a photo.

One day the next-door neighbor, Ruhsar, left her baby with Bayan Nermin. "I've got to go to Aksaray, sister," she explained, "I've fed her, her diaper's clean, I won't be more than two hours." She was the wife of Rıza the printer, newly married. Bayan Nermin accepted with pleasure the request of this young woman who rarely if ever spoke. Ruhsar brought the baby over, laid her on the sofa, and covered her face with a white muslin cloth edged with crocheted lace. "You just go on with whatever you're doing, sister," she said, "she won't make a sound." When Ruhsar was gone, Bayan Nermin worried about the seemingly lifeless baby, that she wouldn't be able to breathe under the muslin cover. She gently lifted a corner of the cloth. Immediately the baby woke up and began to cry. She quickly dropped the muslin back over the child's face, but she wouldn't shut up. She picked her up and cradled her, but her cries only grew louder and louder. Just then Bayan Nermin felt a warmth on her arms: a wet, yellow spot had appeared on the baby's swaddling clothes and was spreading. Not knowing what to do, she put the baby back on the sofa. The baby's ceaseless howls seemed to rock the shanty to its foundations.

The yellow spot had begun to spread over the sofa too. Bayan Nermin ran off, heated some water, fetched a basin, placed the water in it, gathered some towels and other cloths, and took all of this to the baby. When she undid the swaddling clothes, a smell the likes of which she had never before encountered filled the air. From among the dirty diaper and towels its tiny pink belly and coochie emerged, its "there" looked like a large yellow mussel removed from its shell. The baby was sticky all over, a yellow liquid trickled from her groin to her plump legs and from there down to her heels. Bayan Nermin grabbed her by the armpits and plunged her in and out of the basin several times, then she wrapped her in clean towels and put her down again. The child's chin trembled; Bayan Nermin pulled a cover over her. She was out of sorts from fear and agitation. She gently parted the towels from time to time to discover that the baby, now silent, her chin still quivering, had dirtied herself with yellow liquid yet again. She forgot to be disgusted. She found old sheets, old cloths, ripped them up and placed the strips under the baby's bottom, picking up the sticky soiled ones in her hands, over and over. When the baby's mother returned, she found Bayan Nermin and the baby both in tears. She wrapped the baby up as she was and carried her away. "I'm sorry, sister," she said as she left. Bayan Nermin stood aghast at the woman's indifference.

As soon as her husband was back, Bayan Nermin sent him to check on the baby, there was nothing to worry about, but she had him pick up some medicine for her. She looked in on the baby daily, cooked food for her, worried about her. She and the mother had started to become friends. She loved the child as though she had half raised her herself. Bayan Nermin had the baby in her arms one day and was smoking a ciga-rette as she talked with Ruhsar. In the yard, in the warmth of late afternoon, she was off her guard and talked freely, as though to her husband or to some party member. When the young woman heard Bayan Nermin expound on the topic of "God never having been of any help to the poor and needy," she jumped up and grabbed her baby. "Repent, Nermin Abla. Repent, or He shall smite you," she said and then fled, never to return. Not even on those long, bleak evenings when snow fell . . .

For a long time after that, Bayan Nermin was careful not to refer to God in conversations with her neighbors. Her themes instead were cooking, sewing, housecleaning, and the weather. But these were rapidly exhausted. The neighbors seemed interested neither in the recipes described by their Nermin Abla nor in trying them out for themselves. They filed into her kitchen in groups of two or three, announcing, "We hear you got a machine, sister, thought we'd come see it," and then they watched with astonishment the instrument that sliced hard-boiled eggs using a serrated blade; the knives that cut potatoes into little squares, long strips, or thin, round chips; the fantas-tical arms of the machine used to mix cake batter, cookies, and biscuit dough, and then, pulling at the corners of their head-scarves to secure them beneath their chins, they left. Watching them leave without speaking another word, Bayan Nermin's heart would become heavy. *I wonder what they are thinking,* she asked herself. *These people of mine, who are neither amicable nor hostile, neither distant nor close, what is it, I wonder, that they think? The way they look at me, I sense neither friendship nor enmity. Do they know that I want them to understand me, to love me? Do they know that I wish to share with them not only what I hold in my hands but also that which is in my heart?* With these thoughts she stood at the gate, looking long and longingly at the backs of the women retreating from her.

Toward the end of that year, Bayan Nermin got an inkling of what their thoughts were. Someone went by, a person she didn't know but a face she had seen often around the coffee-house. The garden gate was open. Bayan Nermin sprawled on the deck chair she'd placed beneath the plum tree, by the piano, looking first at the sky, then at the tiny shanties that lined three sides of the hill beyond the garden, before finally turning her gaze back to the sky above.

The book she had intended to read lay in her lap. The day was about to end. A solid blueness was descending, growing dense in the middle of the sky. The young man sauntered down the road, past Ruhsar's house. When he reached Bayan Nermin's garden gate he turned his head, and their eyes met. He stood in his tracks, as if struck by lightning. Bayan Nermin instinctively straightened up from her reclining position. The young man suddenly shot a contemptuous jet of saliva straight into the garden toward her deck chair, then continued on his way without a second glance. He was a tall, skinny young man in ratty clothing. Bayan Nermin paid no mind, she raised her head and looked to the sky, fixing her eyes on the blueness, which had grown thicker, darker. *Poor guy, must be another of my duped people,* she thought. *One of the unemployed, to be sure, but if he knew that I'd like to find him a job and that I wish for him to be happy, would he have spat at me?*

By the beginning of winter, Bayan Nermin's people, men and women alike, had begun asking each other what on earth these depraved people were doing here in *their* neighborhood, what business this attractive, well-off woman of indeterminable origin—a broad who dresses like a prostitute, gathers all sorts of curs in her yard and romps about with them, inviting even their own husbands to join the fray, spending hours on end drinking with the men and keeping them entertained, whose peals of laughter jolted even the lads asleep in the houses at the bottom of the hill from their beds—and that cuckolded husband of hers had in their neighborhood. Bayan Nermin threw herself facedown onto the bed. An unbearable pain stabbed her in the stomach. She rang the bell. The floor attendant appeared instantly, and for a moment she was at a loss for words, but she quickly pulled herself together. "Is there a doctor here?" she asked. "No, sister, but one can be found," the attendant responded, turned around, and left. Bayan Nermin smiled lovingly after him and sat up, her stomach pain gone.

—

—And since when is it a sign of superiority to remain a spectator to the indignities inflicted upon the people? she'd asked her husband. Their arguments had become more frequent over the last months. His coolheaded responses never failed to exasperate Bayan Nermin, and this time, too, he maintained full control of his composure:

—If there is one among you who knows what the people really want, let him come forth! He set to filling his pipe, packing the tobacco firmly. Do you think for a moment that you can seduce a bunch of creatures with B.C. heads and thirteenth-century ways of living by telling them that they're being exploited, that every step they take is in the wrong direction, that fasting and saying their prayers are of no use to them?

—Seduce! Seduce! Bayan Nermin jumped to her feet. This was the evening she'd been spat at in the yard. That's not the sort of terminology you used back before the opportunists ripped the party to pieces! Look here, she said to her husband, who was calmly billowing smoke toward the sooty ceiling of the shanty's living room. Look here, first of all, those people you refer to as "creatures"—they are far superior to *you*, sir, with all your knowledge and skills. She thought of the spittle in the garden. She'd gone back and taken a long look, the spittle was white and foamy, as though ejected with vehemence.

Bay Bedri laughed irritably:

—In what way?

—In every way—don't interrupt me—and secondly, more shameful still, why didn't you, as an intellectual possessing so many rightful views about the people, join the party and try to be useful? Why didn't you want to contribute to destroying this exploitative system? But no, just like a counterrevolutionary, an enemy of the people, you . . .

—Oh, come now, enough parroting, Bay Bedri said, again puffing on his pipe. His manner contained the kind of lofty tolerance displayed toward the mentally ill.

—Do you know what they call you? A traitor, that's what they call you . . .

—Now, that's enough, Bay Bedri said, springing to his feet, ripping the pipe from his mouth and flinging it against the window where his wife stood. Bayan Nermin recoiled at the sound of the shattering glass. She sank onto the sofa, onto the very spot that had been soiled by the baby, where the stain remained, and she could not open her mouth. I'm fed up with your passionate whims, of you playing the hero, of you humiliating yourself in front of a bunch of imbeciles you call *the people*, of you amusing yourself by ridiculing them. I'm sick and tired of having to heat water in a tin can in order to bathe, of living in this filth, under a leaking roof, all because of these imbeciles, I've had it up to here with the neighbors and the party members, do you understand? And most of all, I loathe going to bed every blessed night with a woman who buries her head in a pillow of Leninist horsefeathers, do you understand?..

Bayan Nermin came to back her senses at the thundering sound of a running motor, which rattled the entire neighborhood out of its sleep. She was trembling from head to foot. Shards of glass were spread across the sofa. "Opportunist," she hissed. She was alone in the shanty. Next door, at Rıza the printer's house, a light was on.

Whenever Bayan Nermin thought of that night, she felt the same ache in her stomach. But what pained her most of all was the question how, how it could possibly be that she did not know this person, this man she'd gone to bed with, kissed, and loved in every way for so many years—"Your beloved people, who you say are so vastly superior to me, do you know what they really are? They are human beings who listen to the radio with their brains still stuck in the age before writing was even invented. They're still domesticating the camel, the horse, the ox—or no, they haven't even gotten that far yet: they're still learning how to light a fire. What do you know? You! You, what do you know about human beings? Have you ever even been outside of Istanbul? Is it on journeys to Europe that you've learned what these people are like? Vastly superior to me, ha! Have you any idea how man arrived at today's civilization? How many thousands of years have passed since the

217

Stone Age . . . And you, you think you're going to raise *these* people to *my* caliber in just a matter of years? You think you're going to rope me in, patent me to your cause with *their* mindset? . . 'They're many, we're few; they grovel in misery while we enjoy ourselves,' that's what you say. Well, let them not grovel, let them rise to the top, then, but what about their brains, huh, what about their brains? Do they have the mind for it? Do they have the knowledge? 'The Russians've done it, Castro's done it, Mao's done it,' you say . . . Alright, then what keeps your lot from doing it, huh? Why do your 'beloved people' squirm about on the ground like worms? Why don't they pull themselves up, why don't they hold their heads high, why do they stare at the tips of their shoes when they talk, still bowing and scraping when they enter my presence? Most of the time we can't even understand what they're saying, we can't understand what they're talking about, what they're asking for! And these are the people you want to rule us? They're vastly superior to me, huh? Fools! If you want pity for them, I'll give you alms, but if you want esteem and deference, that's quite another story."

Bayan Nermin marveled that she heard him out, that she didn't attack him even if it meant getting beaten up herself, that she did nothing at all to this man who so easily tolerated the suffering of others—and at this she would marvel till her dying day . . . he must have been very frightened, she'd never seen her husband like that before, he was an altogether different man that evening . . .

—

There was a knock at the door. The floor attendant entered.

—Sister, the doctor is skiing. I sent word up the run. He'll see you as soon as he's back.

—Thank you, it doesn't matter now, though: the pain in my stomach has gone away!

—May it not return, sister.

—Thank you. I wonder, if it's not too much trouble, could you help me take these ski boots off? I can't bend over far enough to reach them . . .

—Very well, sister.

Bayan Nermin looked down at the kneeling man's disheveled hair, which looked as if it had been pillaged by an invading army. It was so stiff, each strand stood straight up, piercing the air like an arrow. "What's your name?" she asked with feigned curiosity, as she presented her other foot.

—My name's Medain, sister, originally, but here they find it easier to call me Fedai.

—Where are you from, originally?

—We immigrated from Bulgaria, we were farmers there. I was a year and a half old when we came here.

—How old are you now?

—I was born in '39. My father died three months ago, we weren't able to look after him properly.

—Why not?

—He died before the village headman could issue him an indigent certificate so we could take him to the hospital.

—What was wrong with him?

—Water on his left lung.

Having finished his task, the man stood up.

—Thank you.

—You're welcome . . . I can't forget it, sister: before he died, he told me, "I've been your father all this time, now you must be my father and not hand me over to strangers . . ." The man's eyes welled up with tears.

Bayan Nermin looked at him blankly. She'd heard thousands of tales like his. She was no longer surprised by them, or saddened, she merely listened.

—Are you married?

—I've a wife and two sons.

—May they live long lives!

—Thank you, sister. The older one started school this year. He's been going for six months now, but he still can't read, sister.

Bayan Nermin lit a cigarette and offered one to the man, who put it in his pocket.

—Did you go to school?

—No, sister, I never went to school. We were peasants, what use was school to us! Well, I may not have got an education, but hopefully my boys will, so they don't end up stupid like me, sister!

—Don't speak like that!

—If only I could see the boy through school, though, sister!

—How much do you earn?

—Five or six hundred a month, thank God.

—Why do you thank God?

The man clasped his hands together in a pose of respect.

—I make five thousand a month, and I can barely get by on that.

—Eh, may God keep our country in abundance. It's obvious you're different. I learned to read some when I was in the army, you know, but I've already forgotten how. It's too late for me, now I just want my son to get an education, sister!

—He can't, Bayan Nermin replied heatedly, as if wishing to egg the man on. In this system, with that salary, you can't possibly put your children through school!

—Well then, what am I supposed to do, I mean, when there's no one to turn to!

They eyed each other carefully.

—That is for *you* people to figure out. *We* haven't a care in the world. You see the people here, do you not!

Bayan Nermin opened the wardrobe to choose her dining attire and began sifting through her options. The wardrobe was jam-packed full of clothes of every color. Fedai was transfixed by all the sweaters, the coats, the trousers.

Bayan Nermin couldn't decide what to wear. She pulled out a shiny blouse.

—They said two skeins would be enough, but it was only enough for half!

—Half of what?

—He's a small boy, they said two skeins would be enough . . .

—?..

—My wife was knitting a sweater, but she ran out of yarn
before she could make the whole thing, so she unrav-
eled it and made it a little smaller, but still it wasn't
enough yarn. I got another skein, but now there's not
enough to finish the sleeves...

Holding up a blouse of silvery white lace, Bayan Nermin
turned around and glared at the man. She shuddered to think,
was this man with the disheveled hair and scruffy beard, his
mouth and eyes invisible for the forest of black whiskers,
this child of the Republic born in '39, this brute with slop-
ing shoulders and bowed legs, was he really prepared to settle
all accounts in exchange for the merciful donation of a mere
wool sweater? Then why on earth had he gone on about "when
there's no one to turn to!"?

Bayan Nermin snapped angrily:

—Now, you look here, and look good: I paid six hundred
liras for this, that's a whole month's salary for you, and
all the men and women you see around here, every single one of them has at least two thousand liras worth of
clothing on their backs at any given moment. Do you
understand what I am trying to say? Do you?

The man looked at the blouse being held in front of his
nose and reached out as though to touch it. Bayan Nermin
whisked it back. The man's hand remained hanging in the air
for a brief moment. Bayan Nermin suddenly became aware of
this white hand, broad like a fig leaf. It was covered in delicate
skin like the pink-white cheeks of Ruhsar's baby, the fingers

were long, the cuticles black. Bayan Nermin found herself caught in a revery, imagining a bank manager, or a holding executive starting here as a hotel attendant . . .

—If you like, I'll give you this to take to your wife, what do you say? If you like, you can have everything in this wardrobe. But then . . . Then what will happen? What will you do then? What will become of your children?

A giant, whitish tongue emerged from amid the whiskers to lick his lips, and he again clasped his hands respectfully.

Only Allah is too great to fall. Look at what we were, see what we've become. May those responsible know a worse fate than ours . . . My father had his own farm. He owned property. Oh, and what property it was, you best believe me: ten cows, twenty buffalo, thirty-three oxen, forty-one calves, one hundred and eighty-four hens, two hundred pullets, thirty-one roosters . . . Geese and turkeys, lakes and forests, green-headed ducks, whitewashed houses—a whole village. And at the bottom of a large garden, with a road in front of it, a giant hotel that he ran . . . Then the men came. "This magnificent farm, blessing of God, all this property, this hotel, how come they're yours?" they said, then they took it all away and beat my father. "Tell us where you hid the gold," they demanded, but they couldn't get him to tell. He had so much gold, my father, but they couldn't beat it out of him. They set up two large cauldrons in the garden, one with boiling and one with ice-cold water, they grabbed my father and stripped him naked, and then they plunged him first in one and then in the other cauldron, first in one, and then in the other. That's when my father finally told them where the gold was: it was inside the earthenware pickle jar. They took it all. They told him, "You can run the hotel, but that's all, your sole duty. You'll make your living from what you earn from the hotel, and you'll give us half of that, too."

—So a great big holding, huh! Bayan Nermin said.

The man looked at her, puzzled.

—I beg your pardon? he said. He'd joined his hands together again as he said this. Bayan Nermin noticed the deep cracks on those giant white hands. *My hands were chapped and cracked like that during the year in the shanty, and how they hurt, oh, how they hurt,* she thought to herself.

—You can't educate your children, not in this system we've got, she said to the man.

Her voice was sincere.

—Well, I'm always on duty on this floor. Call me if you need anything, sister.

Bayan Nermin followed Fedai to the door, locking it behind him. The silver-trimmed blouse was still in her hand. She flung it onto the floor, closed the window, and took off her clothes. She stepped on the blouse on her way to lie down on the bed . . .

Winter had come early that year. The snow remained piled in front of the shanty for days. From time to time, Rıza the printer knocked on the snowy windowpane and asked, "Need anything, sister?" Not one other single person, not a single one of God's souls knocked on her door. Within the span of just a few days, those few days when she was snowed in, Bayan Nermin felt like years had passed, with just her and her battery-powered radio, her books, and her thoughts, and that she had grown old and useless. She was awakened one night by strange noises. She could make nothing of these sounds that had pierced the walls of darkness to reach her. She fell back asleep. Later, one morning the sun appeared at last. It quickly melted away all the snow that had covered the doorway, the garden, the windows, and the walls. The running water turned everything to mud. Cheerfully Bayan Nermin opened the door: before her eyes extended a flat, empty marsh. Everything had disappeared. The rotting fence that surrounded the yard, the vines, the acacia, the pomegranate tree, the stunted plum tree, and her piano—they had all disappeared. She moved forward; the thick bass strings of the piano lay tangled like snakes in the slush. The treble strings had disappeared. The sawed-off trunk of the plum tree stood out like a muddy wart. When things got a little drier, she began to search for the piano keys, those marvelous ivory keys. She collected them one by one, washed them in soapy water, dried them with a towel, then with the mournfulness of one saving the ashes of a deceased lover, she placed them in several empty Philip Morris packs, after which she put them and a few articles of clothing in a suitcase and returned to her mother's house. All the way there, she thought of how she'd had so many pleasant experiences, and again and again she forced herself to smile. She told her mother that she now knew the people a little better and that she loved them all the more.

—

She got up, opened the window, and looked down again. The two boys were gone. The snow was grooved and hollow where they had thrashed about. She could distinguish two crooked shadows sliding down from the top of the mountain, getting larger as they approached the bottom. When they were nearer, she saw it was the daughter-in-law of the Özsüt Milk Puddings family and her skiing instructor. He'd been the young woman's lover for years, while her husband lived with the younger daughter-in-law of the Mitrani family. "Perhaps the same doctor's treating all of us!" Bayan Nermin laughed. The lights of the hall on the main floor downstairs and the noise made by its high-society revelers echoed against the snow. The mountain stood straight and tall, concealing the scars on its surface with the freshly falling snow.

She shut the window, pulled the curtains, turned on the light as she made her way to the bed, encountered her half-naked self in the full-length mirror. Not daring to meet the eyes of this forceful woman who always observed her from the mirror and who sometimes exhibited an almost insane fastidiousness in moral matters, she stood and bowed her head, directing her gaze at her toes, as Fedai had, clasped her hands before her belly, and in a trembling voice asked, "Am I on the right path, am I getting closer to my people?" The woman gave Bayan Nermin a belittling look, then reached out her hands to caress her naked body, her thin waist, the semicircular creases of her belly, her throat, her arms, her shrunken, sagging breasts. She quivered at the memory of Bedri sucking those breasts, kissing them, and inhaling their perfume.

She hadn't allowed him near her in the first days of their marriage. When they were alone, when they retired to their bedroom, he would throw himself on her, clutch her with all his might, and ejaculate upon her. Bayan Nermin would wash her dampened skirts again and again, full of disgust. Being a woman wasn't what she had expected, she didn't know what to do or how to do it. She suddenly found herself faced with the nastiness of the whole business. She understood then that her struggle for women's total freedom, her angry discussions, hadn't been conducted for her own sake. She'd simply wanted to oppose an injustice, to show her family, her society, what needed to be done. She'd tried to be a trailblazer, but there was a mistake somewhere in her calculations, and she was trying to identify it. She discussed and debated this with Bedri. The young man would listen, agree with her arguments, then hold her tightly and ejaculate upon her . . .

One morning she told her husband that she knew about the incident with his sister Meral, but that she attached no importance to it at all. They were in bed. He pushed his head between her breasts and burst into sobs, moaning over and over, "You are an angel, I love you so much, never leave me." His tears ran down between her breasts, drenching her belly and farther down still. Bayan Nermin sized up her husband for perhaps the first time. She gently stroked his chestnut hair, his wrestler's neck, his back with its hard, undulating muscles, "It's okay, it doesn't matter, don't worry, no, I won't leave you," she said, then clasped his head, lifted it to hers, and kissed him on the lips. As she kissed him, she was learning how to kiss. Bedri dried his tears on the pillow and gave Nermin a long look. She wrapped her arms around his neck, closed her eyes tightly, and abandoned herself to becoming a woman. One moment a sharp pain took her breath away, the next she was breathing again, she let herself go, at one point she thought she heard a sound, *rrrrip*, her arms fell to her sides, she half opened her eyes and saw Bedri, who had lifted himself on his elbows and was watching her. *Is this how he did it to Meral?* wondered Bayan Nermin, and then she wept. "I didn't hurt you, now, did I darling," Bedri said. She shook her head, kissed her husband, and got out of bed. She was pleased the task was behind her now. It took years for Bayan Nermin to forget the shame and discomfort she felt on those first days and to be able to begin truly making love with her husband. Just when they had begun to understand and respond to each other, and to truly enjoy lovemaking, this matter of *the people* came between them . . .

"Could it be that I am wasting my life, am I that kind of some-one?" Bayan Nermin asked the mirror, her heart sinking. "Could it be that I am, as my mother says, someone who is of no use, to the church or the mosque? Might it be that I am someone who bangs her head against sharp rocks in vain, incurring unhealable wounds with each blow, who walks about letting her blood gush forth claiming, 'Look, see, this society has wounded me yet again,' hoping that society, seeing the blood, will understand its patient, whose chest swells with pride because of her wound, whose self-confidence grows with each new failure as she proclaims, 'Is there another noble person such as me, at odds with her society?', who feels more and more heroic and constantly seeks out new wounds, saying, 'Look, I'm one of those whose toil is changing the world for the better,' while all the time no one is the wiser, no one knows of her wounds or of her heroism, left standing with her labor in her hand? Did we really love each other?" she sighed, looking again at the nipple of her left breast, which was larger than the right; it was Bedri who had discovered this. "Was it really *the people* who came between us, or was Bedri simply tired of me? Did he leave me because my knowledge of the incident with his sister made him feel inferior, or was it only because my breasts had lost their firmness?" When the woman in the mirror commented that it was an aberration, really, to suggest that the people were in any way the reason for her troubles, Bayan Nermin stuck her tongue out at her. "*You* are off your rocker," she said. "I've no time to worry about reasons, anyway—I'm going back to my people, he left me all alone on a mountaintop, never bothered to call and ask how I was getting on, they said Bedri was consorting with blondes, taking them to expensive places. Blondes who belong to the people . . ." She leaned her elbow against the mirror. "What more could one expect of that wannabe boxer, that enemy of the people, that pipe-smoking pig." Her face flushed; for a year now, she'd been evading even the mere thought of another man, and the more she did, the more firmly she fell into the arms of her people. What she could not bring herself to accept, what she simply could not bear, was that she should desire, that she should long for one man and one man only: her husband. Repulsed, she drove this thought from her mind. "I've dedicated myself to the people, I could die for them, from now on there will be no room in my life for personal problems, that's how much I love my people..." she said, pausing at the mention of love, before giving the mirror a shameless wink, then moving closer and pressing her entire body against it. The coolness crushing her breasts, her belly, her thighs, gave her pleasure, she felt a warmth spread from her legs upward, she kissed the woman on the lips, opening her eyes, implored her, "You are an angel, I love you so much, don't leave me." That's when she saw the blouse, which had fallen onto the floor in front of the door. With her hands she pushed her panties down to her knees, wriggled out of them, and then, with the toes of her right foot, flicked the panties up toward the ceiling—they whirled in the air like a delicate jellyfish and fell, wobbling, at the foot of the bed.

Bayan Nermin turned off the overhead light, switched on the bedside lamp, and threw herself headlong onto the bed, burying her head in the feather pillow. "Monsieur Debray, as you can see, I just can't, it's been years, and I'm nearly an old lady now, the people are just so difficult to understand..." she mumbled. Her voice, muffled by the pillow, sounded like the death rattle of someone suffocating. "You're right," agreed Monsieur Debray, "but you, too, are very difficult to understand, and it's also no use feeling sorry . . ." He stroked Bayan Nermin's hair, lifting his arm with difficulty, as though unwell. "Okay, so what did I do wrong? Can you tell me exactly what it is I shouldn't have done?" Bayan Nermin asked, turning toward the young man. "No, no, that's impossible to say!" replied Debray. "What am I to do then?" asked Bayan Nermin. "You know I asked Fidel the same question the other evening—he doesn't like me very much, or rather, he doesn't trust me, he got up and left just as I was about to make my point." "Personally, I don't think you should expect help from anyone," answered Monsieur Debray. "No one can save you, you must cut your own umbilical cord." And he stood up and stumbled toward the door . . . Once left alone, "Look at that little bastard now, would you," Bayan Nermin grumbled, "where does he get off offering advice to a woman old enough to be his mother, if he had any sense, he would have used it on himself . . ." At that moment her doctor came to mind, so young and handsome, but then his life was right on track, Bayan Nermin thought. Flocks of patients bided their time out in his waiting room. *People whose lives are on track, they can't possibly understand me, and, besides, I don't even know him all that well.* "He gets along with everybody!" she yelled into the middle of the room. *Well then, who is it going to be?* she asked herself, marching a procession of people she knew before her eyes, one by one, but none suited her fancy: there was that one from her adolescence, but she couldn't even recall his face just then . . . All of a sudden she thought of Ilyich; embarrassed she reached out and switched off the lamp. At that moment, she came nose to nose with Joseph, and they both laughed, he was the only man she'd gotten together with, now and then, since Bedri. She snuggled up to him lustfully, hiding her face, burying it in his firm chest. "We're on our own again Joseph, without a party, we're a mess, we're in pieces," she complained. Joseph seized Bayan Nermin by the hair and lifted her head off his chest, and they stayed like that, face-to-face. "You all rolled up your pants before you even caught sight of the stream!" he said. Bayan Nermin was like a child afraid of being punished. "It's not my fault, I did everything I could," the words volleyed from her mouth, "I went among my people, but I couldn't bridge a gap of centuries just like that. And the people are a tough nut to crack, very tough, but I won't give up, you know me, they will not make me stray from the path . . ." "I know you won't!" Joseph said, squeezing her neck affectionately, then he laid his head on the pillow, stretched out beside her. "Do you know, you are the only person who truly understands me," the young woman said, kissing his cheek. "And what are you going to do now?" asked the man, leaning over her. He seemed to worry about her in a friendly way, but when he spoke his breath struck her lips, making her shudder. "I don't know," she murmured, as though to herself. "The people are tough, very tough, do you hear me, Joseph, I talk to you as I would to myself, I'm not going to contend that I'm able to love them, because love is something else altogether, something concrete, I might love someone—say, my mother or you—but to say that I love a whole mass of people I don't know, all of them at once, sounds like nonsense to me. 'You must love everyone'—that was a measurement of honor for the generations before us. A slogan of the intellectuals, a brief phrase to be memorized. I AM OBLIGED TO LOVE ALL PEOPLE. Obliged, I say, because so long as they're not free, neither am I. This is a calculation on my part, a profit perhaps. But derived from awareness, not virtue alone, not the kind of behavior meant to give the recipient a feeling of obligation. I will fight for humanity, dedicate a lifetime to the fight. I may be proved right or wrong in the end, I will dedicate myself to making people lovable, but I'd be ashamed to say that I do this because I love them. Do you understand me? . ."

"*That* is true love!" the man said, pulling the woman's body to his and kissing her throat. "In the phrase 'I love all people,'" continued Bayan Nermin impudently, "I sense a shamelessness, an impertinence even, I can't quite put my finger on it!" "My obstinate girl," said Joseph, touching his lips to her nose and letting them rest there a moment. "I may be obstinate," giggled Bayan Nermin, "but I'm not a traitor like you." And then she gave him a long kiss on the mouth before he could respond. "Come with me, I'm going to take to the road, go far away into the 'heartland,'" she said. "Impossible," said the man, raining kisses on her body. His bristly hair rubbed against her chin, throat, shoulders. "But why not?" she asked fearfully. "What is it—are you bored with me, don't you love me?" "I'm not bored, and I do love you," the man huffed. "I love you, but I can't come with you. Do it on your own." "But I want to be with you," she insisted. "Joseph," she said, "listen to me: I'm getting older, I'm tired, now and then I get this feeling of fear, I've always been alone, I've never had anyone to help me, but now I'd like to share the future with someone I get along with, someone I love, to share with them all that's left to live. Before I die, I want to see . . ." "These things can't be rushed," laughed Joseph, dropping his head on her belly. She stroked his prickly hair against the grain. "What do you mean, rushed," she laughed, "when you did it, weren't you in a rush?" The man lifted his head to hers and looked straight into her eyes. "We did it at exactly the right time," he told her, covering her lips with his. She cried out as though in pain, struggled under the might of his masterful body, he pressed down on her with persistent, renewed passion until she was unable to move, she dug her nails into the weight, pulling it close against her. "How beautiful you are!" she moaned, "Traitorous and boorish and cruel and affectionate, all at the same time. I can't give you up, I just can't. Don't leave me, please, don't leave me." "More, more," the man said, and, shaking, he buried his face between her breasts. Bayan Nermin turned her head left and right, her body moved up and down, first slowly and then faster, and like an octopus it began to open and close. At this moment she was like a harmonica that played itself without making a sound. In a barely audible voice she moaned, "Joseph! Bedri! Bedri! Joseph!" and then she raised herself up and threw herself down onto the bed again and again until at last she froze still, a lump of black rose made of cloud.

The purplish light of the snow seeped in through the openings in the curtains, illuminating Bayan Nermin's right arm, which dangled from the bed, and her left arm, with which she had tightly pressed the feather pillow against her breast but which now rested limply upon it. This side of her face was bright white-blue, while the other was pitch-black. She was now like one of her beloved people, one of those who no longer even wished to be liberated from the suffering they'd endured for centuries. Bayan Nermin picked up the blouse from the floor, found a pair of lamé trousers to match, dressed, brushed her hair, looked in the mirror at her swollen lips, then pressed the bell. Fedai immediately appeared at the door. "It's you again?" she asked. For some reason she'd thought she'd never see him again. "Tell them to send me a whiskey soda and a sandwich." Opening the curtains, she pressed her forehead against the window and began to wait. The whiteness of the darkness, like an abyss, had enveloped the hotel. For a moment she felt herself plummeting, swept up by the vortex that bored into the center of the abyss. She quickly turned around, leaning back against the window, and faced the door. It was ajar, and Fedai was entering the room with a tray, and with him the hubbub from the hall below. "Put it down there," she directed. A heavy smell filled the room as he approached. "What's that awful smell?" Bayan Nermin said, glancing about. She saw the hair of the man standing before her, oiled, combed, parted at one side, sticky and shining. His tiny black eyes traveled over her blouse then leapt down to her trousers, like moths nibbling at the silver threads. That feeling that had seized Bayan Nermin as she stood before the police years ago when she was taken into the station; a fear swept over her, *What if he tries to rape me? Or has he been watching me all this time?* Furrowing her brows, "Tell them downstairs I want them to ring me at six tomorrow morning," she said.

"Very well, sister, but why so early?"

"Just because, another journey has come up."

" . . . . . "

"Alright?"

"Alright, sister . . . Sister, so you mean to say my boy can't get an education, then?"

"Why on earth does it matter so much to you that he get an education!"

"Well, so he can make something of himself, sister, be a government worker somewhere, not have to rough it like me."

If it were up to these people, the whole of Turkey would consist of one vast civil-service class, she laughed to herself, then took a sip of whiskey.

"Well, perhaps he will get an education, if it's Allah's will, perhaps he'll become a civil servant, or a supervisor somewhere. You go on now, I'll ring if I need anything."

"Very well, sister, as you wish."

He left the room. Bayan Nermin's words echoed from wall to wall and burst upon her own ears: "If it's Allah's will! Allah willing! If it's Allah's will! If it's Allah's will!" She drained the glass of whiskey, and a flush of resolution spread across her face. "How else was I supposed to speak with our Medain now, Joseph?" she said, bursting into laughter.

Bayan Nermin pulled the clothes out of the wardrobe and began placing them in the suitcase that had carried her belongings from Taşlıtarla to her mother's house, putting the flimsy, frilly ones aside for Fedai's wife. "I won't be wearing these anymore, Joseph, I'm going to the heartland, deep into the heartland, back to my people." She stood up straight. She looked into the mirror, smiling. She was pleased with herself.

To the woman across from her she asked, "YOU, I WONDER, DO *YOU* LOVE ALL THE PEOPLE?"

Glossary of Turkish Honorifics

Abla "older sister," a term of respect for women older than oneself, used after the first name.

Ağabey "older brother," a term of respect for men older than oneself, used, like "Abla," after the first name.

Ağbi an abbreviated form of "Ağabey."

Bay a term used after the first or the last name, traditionally in reference to wealthy, powerful men. This usage gained prevalence after the founding of the republic in 1923 as an equivalent for Western forms of address such as Mr.

Bayan a term used for women, after the first or the last name. The word, derived from "Bay," was created after the founding of the republic in 1923, as an equivalent for Western forms of address such as Mrs./Ms.

Bey a respectful form of address for men, used after the first name.

Efendi a courteous title, akin to "sir," used after a man's first name.

Hanım a form of address used for adult women, after the first name, roughly equivalent to "Ms."

Leylâ Erbil was one of the most influential Turkish writers of the late twentieth and early twenty-first centuries, Leylâ Erbil (1931–2013) was a renowned, innovative literary stylist who tackled issues at the heart of what it means to be human, in mind and body. Erbil ventured where few writers dare to tread, turning her lens upon the tides of social norms and the shaping of identities, getting down to the nitty-gritty of emotional conflict, and plumbing the depths of history and human psyche.

Erbil was twice nominated by Turkey PEN for the Nobel Prize for Literature, becoming the first woman writer from Turkey to achieve that distinction. Her novel *A Strange Woman* is one of three works recommended for translation by the Turkish National Committee for UNESCO. Erbil's work has been the subject of dozens of theses, and several symposia, including *Ethics and Aesthetics in the Works of Leylâ Erbil*, held at Bilgi University in Istanbul in 2006, to commemorate the author's fiftieth year of writing. In 2013, Erbil was invited as guest of honor for the 2013 Cunda International Workshop for the Translation of Turkish Literature (CWTTL).

Amy Marie Spangler hails from small-town southern Ohio but has lived in Istanbul for over twenty years. Cofounder and director of AnatoliaLit Agency, she has published several translations and is working to expand her oeuvre in the coming years. She is one of three translators collectively laboring on a translation of Leylâ Erbil's *What Remains*, forthcoming from Deep Vellum.

PARTNERS

pixel ||| texel

ADDITIONAL DONORS, CONT'D

Mark Haber
Mary Cline
Maynard Thomson
Michael Reklis
Mike Soto
Mokhtar Ramadan
Nikki & Dennis Gibson
Patrick Kukucka
Patrick Kutcher
Rev. Elizabeth & Neil Moseley
Richard Meyer

Scott & Katy Nimmons
Sherry Perry
Sydneyann Binion
Stephen Harding
Stephen Williamson
Susan Carp
Susan Ernst
Theater Jones
Tim Perttula
Tony Thomson

SUBSCRIBERS

Margaret Terwey
Ben Fountain
Gina Rios
Elena Rush
Courtney Sheedy
Caroline West
Brian Bell
Charles Dee Mitchell
Cullen Schaar
Harvey Hix
Jeff Lierly
Elizabeth Simpson

Nicole Yurcaba
Jennifer Owen
Melanie Nicholls
Alan Glazer
Michael Doss
Matt Bucher
Katarzyna Bartoszynska
Michael Binkley
Erin Kubatzky
Martin Piñol
Michael Lighty
Joseph Rebella

Jarratt Willis
Heustis Whiteside
Samuel Herrera
Heidi McElrath
Jeffrey Parker
Carolyn Surbaugh
Stephen Fuller
Kari Mah
Matt Ammon
Elif Ağanoğlu

AVAILABLE NOW FROM DEEP VELLUM

SHANE ANDERSON · *After the Oracle* · USA

MICHÈLE AUDIN · *One Hundred Twenty-One Days* · translated by Christiana Hills · FRANCE

BAE SUAH · *Recitation* · translated by Deborah Smith · SOUTH KOREA

MARIO BELLATIN · *Mrs. Murakami's Garden* · translated by Heather Cleary · *Beauty Salon* · translated by David Shook · MEXICO

EDUARDO BERTI · *The Imagined Land* · translated by Charlotte Coombe · ARGENTINA

CARMEN BOULLOSA · *Texas: The Great Theft* · *Before* · *Heavens on Earth*
translated by Samantha Schnee · Peter Bush · Shelby Vincent · MEXICO

MAGDA CARNECI · *FEM* · translated by Sean Cotter · ROMANIA

LEILA S. CHUDORI · *Home* · translated by John H. McGlynn · INDONESIA

MATHILDE CLARK · *Lone Star* · translated by Martin Aitken · DENMARK

SARAH CLEAVE, ed. · *Banthology: Stories from Banned Nations* ·
IRAN, IRAQ, LIBYA, SOMALIA, SUDAN, SYRIA & YEMEN

LOGEN CURE · *Welcome to Midland: Poems* · USA

ANANDA DEVI · *Eve Out of Her Ruins* · translated by Jeffrey Zuckerman · MAURITIUS

PETER DIMOCK · *Daybook from Sheep Meadow* · USA

CLAUDIA ULLOA DONOSO · *Little Bird*, translated by Lily Meyer · PERU/NORWAY

RADNA FABIAS · *Habitus* · translated by David Colmer · CURAÇAO/NETHERLANDS

ROSS FARRAR · *Ross Sings Cheree & the Animated Dark: Poems* · USA

ALISA GANIEVA · *Bride and Groom* · *The Mountain and the Wall*
translated by Carol Apollonio · RUSSIA

FERNANDA GARCIA LAU · *Out of the Cage* · translated by Will Vanderhyden · ARGENTINA

ANNE GARRÉTA · *Sphinx* · *Not One Day* · *In/concrete* · translated by Emma Ramadan · FRANCE

JÓN GNARR · *The Indian* · *The Pirate* · *The Outlaw* · translated by Lytton Smith · ICELAND

GOETHE · *The Golden Goblet: Selected Poems* · *Faust, Part One*
translated by Zsuzsanna Ozsváth and Frederick Turner · GERMANY

SARA GOUDARZI · *The Almond in the Apricot* · USA

NOEMI JAFFE · *What are the Blind Men Dreaming?* · translated by Julia Sanches & Ellen Elias-Bursac · BRAZIL

CLAUDIA SALAZAR JIMÉNEZ · *Blood of the Dawn* · translated by Elizabeth Bryer · PERU

PERGENTINO JOSÉ · *Red Ants* · MEXICO

TAISIA KITAISKAIA · *The Nightgown & Other Poems* · USA

SONG LIN · *The Gleaner Song: Selected Poems* · translated by Dong Li · CHINA

JUNG YOUNG MOON · *Seven Samurai Swept Away in a River* · *Vaseline Buddha*
translated by Yewon Jung · SOUTH KOREA

KIM YIDEUM · *Blood Sisters* · translated by Ji yoon Lee · SOUTH KOREA

JOSEFINE KLOUGART · *Of Darkness* · translated by Martin Aitken · DENMARK

YANICK LAHENS · *Moonbath* · translated by Emily Gogolak · HAITI

FOUAD LAROUI · *The Curious Case of Dassoukine's Trousers* · translated by Emma Ramadan · MOROCCO

MARIA GABRIELA LLANSOL · *The Geography of Rebels Trilogy: The Book of Communities; The Remaining Life; In the House of July & August* translated by Audrey Young · PORTUGAL

PABLO MARTÍN SÁNCHEZ · *The Anarchist Who Shared My Name* · translated by Jeff Diteman · SPAIN

DOROTA MASŁOWSKA · *Honey, I Killed the Cats* · translated by Benjamin Paloff · POLAND

BRICE MATTHIEUSSENT· *Revenge of the Translator* · translated by Emma Ramadan · FRANCE

LINA MERUANE · *Seeing Red* · translated by Megan McDowell · CHILE

VALÉRIE MRÉJEN · *Black Forest* · translated by Katie Shireen Assef · FRANCE

FISTON MWANZA MUJILA · *Tram 83* · *The River in the Belly: Selected Poems,* translated by Bret Maney DEMOCRATIC REPUBLIC OF CONGO

GORAN PETROVIĆ · *At the Lucky Hand, aka The Sixty-Nine Drawers* · translated by Peter Agnone · SERBIA

LUDMILLA PETRUSHEVSKAYA· *The New Adventures of Helen: Magical Tales,* translated by Jane Bugaeva · RUSSIA

ILJA LEONARD PFEIJFFER · *La Superba* · translated by Michele Hutchison · NETHERLANDS

RICARDO PIGLIA · *Target in the Night* · translated by Sergio Waisman · ARGENTINA

SERGIO PITOL · *The Art of Flight* · *The Journey* · *The Magician of Vienna* · *Mephisto's Waltz: Selected Short Stories* · *The Love Parade* translated by George Henson · MEXICO

JULIE POOLE · *Bright Specimen: Poems from the Texas Herbarium* · USA

EDUARDO RABASA · *A Zero-Sum Game* · translated by Christina MacSweeney · MEXICO

ZAHIA RAHMANI · *"Muslim": A Novel* · translated by Matthew Reeck · FRANCE/ALGERIA

MANON STEFAN ROS · *The Blue Book of Nebo* · WALES

JUAN RULFO · *The Golden Cockerel & Other Writings* · translated by Douglas J. Weatherford · MEXICO

ETHAN RUTHERFORD · *Farthest South & Other Stories* · USA

TATIANA RYCKMAN · *Ancestry of Objects* · USA

JIM SCHUTZE · *The Accommodation* · USA

OLEG SENTSOV · *Life Went On Anyway* · translated by Uilleam Blacker · UKRAINE

MIKHAIL SHISHKIN · *Calligraphy Lesson: The Collected Stories* translated by Marian Schwartz, Leo Shtutin, Mariya Bashkatova, Sylvia Maizell · RUSSIA

ÓFEIGUR SIGURÐSSON · *Öræfi: The Wasteland* · translated by Lytton Smith · ICELAND

DANIEL SIMON, ED. · *Dispatches from the Republic of Letters* · USA

MUSTAFA STITOU · *Two Half Faces* · translated by David Colmer · NETHERLANDS

SOPHIA TERAZAWA · *Winter Phoenix: Testimonies in Verse* · POLAND

MÄRTA TIKKANEN · *The Love Story of the Century* · translated by Stina Katchadourian · SWEDEN

BOB TRAMMELL · *Jack Ruby & the Origins of the Avant-Garde in Dallas & Other Stories* · USA

BENJAMIN VILLEGAS · *ELPASO: A Punk Story* · translated by Jay Noden · MEXICO

SERHIY ZHADAN · *Voroshilovgrad* · translated by Reilly Costigan-Humes & Isaac Wheeler · UKRAINE

FORTHCOMING FROM DEEP VELLUM

MARIO BELLATIN • *Etchapare* • translated by Shook • MEXICO

CAYLIN CARPA-THOMAS • *Iguana Iguana* • USA

MIRCEA CĂRTĂRESCU • *Solenoid* • translated by Sean Cotter · ROMANIA

TIM COURSEY • *Driving Lessons* • USA

ANANDA DEVI • *When the Night Agrees to Speak to Me* • translated by Kazim Ali • MAURITIUS

DHUMKETU • *The Shehnai Virtuoso* • translated by Jenny Bhatt • INDIA

LEYLÂ ERBIL • *A Strange Woman* • translated by Nermin Menemencioğlu & Amy Marie Spangler· TURKEY

ALLA GORBUNOVA • *It's the End of the World, My Love* • translated by Elina Alter • RUSSIA

NIVEN GOVINDEN • *Diary of a Film* • GREAT BRITAIN

GYULA JENEI · *Always Different* • translated by Diana Senechal · HUNGARY

DIA JUBAILI • *No Windmills in Basra* • translated by Chip Rosetti • IRAQ

ELENI KEFALA • *Time Stitches* • translated by Peter Constantine • CYPRUS

UZMA ASLAM KHAN • *The Miraculous True History of Nomi Ali* • PAKISTAN

ANDREY KURKOV • *Grey Bees* • translated by Boris Dralyuk • UKRAINE

JORGE ENRIQUE LAGE • *Freeway La Movie* • translated by Lourdes Molina • CUBA

TEDI LÓPEZ MILLS • *The Book of Explanations* • translated by Robin Myers • MEXICO

ANTONIO MORESCO • *Clandestinity* • translated by Richard Dixon • ITALY

FISTON MWANZA MUJILA • *The Villain's Dance,* translated by Roland Glasser • DEMOCRATIC REPUBLIC OF CONGO

N. PRABHAKARAN • *Diary of a Malayali Madman* • translated by Jayasree Kalathil • INDIA

THOMAS ROSS • *Miss Abracadabra* • USA

IGNACIO RUIZ-PÉREZ • *Isles of Firm Ground* • translated by Mike Soto • MEXICO

LUDMILLA PETRUSHEVSKAYA • *Kidnapped: A Crime Story,* translated by Marian Schwartz • RUSSIA

NOAH SIMBLIST, ed. • *Tania Bruguera: The Francis Effect* • CUBA

S. YARBERRY • *A Boy in the City* • USA